HOLLYWOOD DREAMS

MAE ARCHER

MELBOURNE, AUSTRALIA

https://www.pishukinpress.com/

First Published 2022

Pishukin Press

Cover design: Created using Canva elements

Previously published 2014 by Momentum

Paperback ISBN: 9781922871213

To my daughter who believes all of my fantastical stories and
can match them with her own.

Chapter 1

Even though Beau Tennant was on busy Melrose Avenue in Los Angeles he'd never felt so alone. As he waited for help, he watched the faces of people passing. They stared straight ahead, or craned their necks to the opposite side of the street to avert their eyes.

That's when he saw her, waist-length brown hair bouncing as she walked. She held a phone to her ear, a big handbag dragged on her wrist, and her other hand clutched a box. Her brown eyes caught his and when she didn't turn away he felt a thrill, as if he'd touched an electricity pole.

She stopped beside him. 'I have to go,' she said.

Beau looked up at her, but her eyes were on the box in her hand.

'I'll be there in twenty minutes.' She hung up and dropped the phone in her bag. 'You're stuck,' she said, looking at the wheelchair caught in a crack of concrete on the sidewalk.

'Yes, ma'am,' Beau drawled in his Southern accent.

'Here, hold this.' She placed the box onto his lap and squatted, somehow making the act look elegant in her silver platforms and black Capri pants. 'Mm,' she murmured. 'I need some grunt to get that wheel out.'

'Don't worry—' he started, but she'd walked off, leaving him with the box. What did she think he was, her shelf?

She stood in the path of the oncoming crowd. He saw her zero in on a young man in a tight, white T-shirt that displayed his bulging pecs. Beau knew the moment that White T-shirt caught her eye.

White T-shirt smiled flirtatiously, and slowed. 'Hey,' he said.

'Hey yourself.' She smiled back. 'So I need a hand with something. You got a few minutes?'

'Sure,' the young man replied.

She led him over to Beau. 'I need you to lift the wheel while I push,' she said firmly.

White T-shirt was taken aback, but her tone obviously brooked no argument.

'There's no need—' Beau tried to interject again, but she paid him no mind as she went to stand behind the chair.

'On my count,' she told the young man. 'One, two, three.' She pushed, while he lifted the wheel. 'Thanks. Appreciate you being a good Samaritan.' She patted White T-shirt on the shoulder and turned to Beau. 'Are you good?'

White T-shirt looked at her for a moment, but apparently realizing he was dismissed he merged back with the crowd, a confused look on his face.

'Yes, ma'am,' Beau said, feeling as confused as the young man who'd helped him. When the woman first stopped he'd pegged her for a Looky-Lou; one of those people who thought they could get his life story as part and parcel of small talk. Yet now that she'd gone and blown his first impression out of the water, he didn't quite know what to make of her.

'What happened here?' She looked at his hand with concern.

He'd cut it on the wheel spoke when he'd tried to wrench the wheelchair out of the crack. Before he could say anything, again, she had taken hold of his hand and was looking closely at the cut.

'It's fine.' He pulled his hand back, feeling self-conscious under the force of her attention.

'You can't turn the wheels with a cut in your hand. You'll get an infection.' She went behind the chair and before he knew what she was doing, she was pushing him toward Luna's Café.

That had been his destination—to meet his friend, Carter—but Beau didn't know whether to feel thankful or annoyed that she was hijacking him and his chair without asking.

She chose a table under a green shade umbrella. After she moved a metal chair out of the way and took the box off his lap, she pushed him in. As she sat across from him their knees almost touched under the small table. She placed the box under her chair, and took hold of his palm again.

'It just needs a good clean.' She rifled through her bag.

A waiter appeared. 'Chai latte with skim milk.' She rattled off her order without looking up.

'And you, sir?' The waiter looked at him.

'Black coffee, no sugar,' he said.

The woman pulled out an antiseptic tube and a box of bandages from her bag. As he watched the gentle way she tended to his wound he was puzzled. She was a stranger who'd jumped in to help him when everyone else acted like he was a leper.

He nodded at her supplies. 'You come prepared.'

'I'm a costume designer,' she said. 'In my line of work I find there's always some minor injury or another that needs to be tended to.'

He should have guessed. Prime Studio was only twenty minutes away and a lot of its employees frequented Luna's for breakfast meetings. It was also a café known for celebrity watching and was stalked by tabloid reporters, which is why Carter insisted they meet here.

'So you're in the business,' he said, stressing the word.

Los Angeles was the city of entertainment. Most people were employed in some way by the entertainment industry and if they weren't, then they were just angling for their 'break.'

'I see that we haven't made a good first impression?' she said. 'But I guess that's not much of a surprise. How long were you stuck there for?'

As she looked at him, Beau saw something he hadn't seen in anyone's eyes since he'd sat in the wheelchair. Understanding. 'Half an hour,' he said. 'Shit, I have to call someone.'

She placed a bandage on his hand, gently pressing down to make sure it stuck. He felt his skin tingle.

'Thanks.' He was feeling nonplussed at the sensations her touch evoked. He got out his cell phone. 'Hey, Carter, no need to come down,' he said quickly. 'I'm okay.' He cut off Carter's questions. 'I'll explain later,' and hung up.

'I guess I should introduce myself.' She offered her hand. 'I'm Maree Reynard.'

'Beau Tennant.' As they shook, her hand was enveloped by his much larger one and he realized how small she was. Her presence and manner made her seem much taller. If they'd met while he was standing up she'd only reach his shoulder.

'Lieutenant? Corporal?' she asked.

He was surprised. He was in civilian duds, wearing jeans and a blue short-sleeved shirt. 'Lieutenant. How did you know?'

She reached across the table and lifted his dog tags. He smelled the sweet scent of her hand cream. As she brushed her thumb across the metal he felt a stirring as if she was brushing his skin.

He'd debated about wearing them this morning. A civilian had no reason to wear dog tags, but Beau felt naked without them.

'New to this?' She nodded at the wheelchair as she released the tags, her fingers like the whisper of a butterfly's wings.

'A week stateside.' Beau had joined up with six of his friends after September 11 and had been in the army ever since.

The waiter returned and placed their coffee orders on the table.

'You're the first person I've met, outside of the hospital, who is nonplussed by my wheelchair.' He took a sip of coffee.

'A friend in high school.' Maree lifted the sugar dispenser and poured in two teaspoons. 'She had a car accident after a party. The first six months she got stuck a few times. It's amazing how many people don't know what to do. The whole wheelchair thing spooks them.'

'But not you?'

'Not much spooks me.'

There was a glimmer of flirtatiousness as Maree looked at him. For a moment he forgot himself and responded as the old him, his lips quirking into a smile, his shoulders straightening as he got ready to launch into his move. Then he saw his reflection in the window behind her. His blond hair hung to his shoulders, a beard covered most of his face, and even his eyes were unrecognizable with their brown tint. He looked down at the table as he took a sip of his coffee. He was imagining it. Why would a woman like her be interested in someone like him?

'What are you doing in town?' she asked.

He rubbed his hand across the back of his neck. He'd practiced his story a thousand times, yet now that it was show time, he felt ill at ease. 'I'm meeting with some people. They might be making a movie about me.'

'Oh,' she said.

He cleared his throat. 'Yeah.'

'Did you write the screenplay?' she asked.

'No, a friend of mine wrote it.' He took a sip of his coffee.

'You're a braver person than I am.'

'Why?' he asked.

'Are you sure you know what you're getting yourself in for? After all Hollywood is not known for its accurate storytelling.'

Beau was surprised by her serious face. Usually women were impressed by his movie credentials, but Maree seemed to be concerned that he was naive in getting involved in the business.

'Well, it's based on me, but they're not using my name,' Beau covered himself, not wanting her to think he was a fame chaser, but a regular Joe Blow who just happened to find himself in extraordinary circumstances.

'That won't make much difference,' she said wryly. 'Once that movie comes out you can kiss a regular life goodbye.'

'You seem to know a lot about the negative effects of fame?' he asked.

'My father is an actor.' She said the word like it was a curse.

'You don't sound like you like actors?' Beau asked, guessing from her formal use of father instead of dad that her relationship was strained.

'Maybe I don't.' Maree laughed wryly. 'I've seen too well what fame can do to people. They become arrogant, self-centered, and lose all touch with reality.'

She was looking down at the table, her eyelashes shading her eyes, but her pain was obvious from the sad slant of her lips.

'Not all actors are like that,' Beau said. 'I've met some and they seem perfectly nice.' Even though he'd been thinking cynically about the movie business, now he was feeling strangely defensive.

'Some.' Maree didn't sound convinced.

'Your twenty minutes are almost up,' he said abruptly. She gave him a blank look. 'You told whoever you were speaking to on the phone that you'd be there in twenty minutes,' he explained.

'Yes.' She looked at her watch. 'You're right. I should get going.'

'I've got it,' he said, as she reached for her purse. 'No, really.' He held her hand down when he saw that she was about to argue.

'Okay,' she agreed, a small smile on her face.

He took out his wallet and placed a note on the table.

'It was nice meeting you, Beau.' Maree stood.

He looked up, noticing the way she said his name with an inflection. 'Nice to meet you too, Maree.'

He hesitated. Normally at this point he'd ask for her number, an act that used to be as natural as breathing, but in this new role it didn't seem right. She lingered, and he saw in her eyes that she was waiting, giving him the chance to ask.

'Would you maybe—' he started, his mouth forming the words of their own volition, but he couldn't finish the sentence. 'Never mind. Thanks for everything.' He wrenched his wheels in the opposite direction.

'Yes,' she said.

He stopped and turned his head.

'Call me.' She handed him a card and leaned down, giving him a soft kiss on his cheekbone above the beard.

After she had been swallowed up by the crowd Beau looked down at the business card she'd passed to him. It was plain white and listed her title as Costume Designer for *The Time of Our Lives*, a popular soap opera that had been on television for thirty odd years and whose speciality was love triangles between various family members and their lovers. Beau didn't know if he would call. Pursuing someone who was so close to the business and who could easily break his cover wasn't prudent, but he was intrigued.

He was still thinking about her when he entered his apartment. He'd never met a woman like Maree. It was refreshing to spend time with someone so warm and natural, without an iota of artifice. He got out of the wheelchair, leaving it by the front door, as he walked into the bedroom. He looked into the vanity mirror as he took off the wig and hung it up on the Styrofoam dummy-head sitting on the table. He carefully poked his eye with his index finger and removed the disposable brown tinted contact lenses and put them in the trash.

When he looked back in the mirror, it was now the face of Tom Calvert staring at him. Tom, with his short, slicked brown hair, the blue eyes that a reporter had once described as icy, and the fine features that had helped him launch a career as a fashion model until he became a 'model slash actor', and then finally an actor only.

Sometimes he looked in the mirror and cursed himself. While his good looks had opened up doors, they'd also closed as many, guaranteeing that he would always be seen as a soap actor first and a serious actor second.

He jumped in the shower, momentarily startled as he started to soap himself and saw the black tattoo snaking across his arms and chest. It was in semi-permanent ink, and proclaimed in cursive script 'For those I love I will sacrifice.'

As Tom stepped out of the shower his phone rang.

'So how did you go?' demanded the voice of his agent, Carter.

'Really well,' Tom said. 'Just have to learn to avoid sketchy sidewalks in the future.'

'Ha ha,' Carter said.

Tom heard the sound of rustling paper and knew that Carter was doing his usual and multitasking as he spoke to him.

'We've got a date for the Marco shoot in a couple of weeks.' Carter reminded him of the sportswear line he'd agree to endorse.

'Great.' Tom faked enthusiasm.

He hadn't wanted to do it. He knew that an endorsement was just another cross against him being taken seriously, but it was the only way to scratch the right back in order to get an audition. The *Heroes of Tennessee* director was married to the CEO of Marco and Carter had negotiated the deal. Thankfully it had worked, and Tom had blown the director away and scored his dream part.

'Only a month until shooting starts. Do you think you'll be ready?' Carter asked.

'Shouldn't be a problem,' Tom said. The movie was about six friends from a small town in Tennessee who signed up to the army on the same day, and Beau's character was based on the only soldier who'd survived. Tom had been in character for a week. He'd spent hours every day as Beau, practicing maneuvering his wheelchair in and out of buildings, onto buses, and out on the street, seeing how people related to him. With each day that passed he'd felt Beau settling onto him like an old coat.

'Good,' Carter said. 'Because you know what's at stake.'

'I know.' This part was going to make his career. He would finally be the serious actor that he'd always wanted to be.

After he hung up he caught sight of Maree's business card and smiled. Here was his chance to really put himself to the test as Beau.

Chapter 2

Maree was pinning a police costume onto a male extra when her cell phone rang. They were shooting a riot scene next week, and there were twenty extras whose costumes had to be fitted. She answered absent-mindedly, pressing her Bluetooth earpiece.

'Maree's phone,' she said, her words mumbled from the pin she was holding between her lips.

'Hi Maree, it's Beau.'

She smiled when she heard his deep Southern accent and slipped the pin out of her mouth.

'We met a few days ago when you helped me out,' he interjected into the silence.

'I remember.' It was exactly three days ago and she'd almost given up on him calling.

Maree had been walking to her car after a morning meeting with a supplier when she'd seen Beau in the middle of the sidewalk, the crowd parting around him like the Red Sea. She'd sensed immediately from the stillness of his posture that something was wrong. When their eyes met, he'd flinched and looked away. She'd quickly searched for the source of his distress, and that's when she noticed the wheelchair was slightly crooked and he was stuck.

'How's the cut?' she asked now. He'd been so nervous when she cleaned his wound, her heart had filled with tenderness at his vulnerability.

'Good, good,' he said. 'How have you been?'

'Run ragged.' Maree told him about the upcoming shoot. 'By this time next week I'm going to run screaming if I see a police officer, which could be dangerous,' she mused. 'After all they do have guns.' She felt a thrill as she heard Beau's rich laugh echo in her ear. 'Have you seen any more of Los Angeles?'

'Not much. I've been sticking close to the hotel I'm staying at,' he said. 'I was hoping you would have dinner with me and help me stretch my horizons.'

'Love to.' Maree smoothed the material around the extra's leg.

'Oh ... good.'

'You sound surprised that I said yes.' She started pinning up the seam.

'No, I'm not surprised,' he said, sounding anything but.

'Really?' Maree countered. 'Because you sound shit-faced scared.'

Beau laughed, the reverberation in her ear filling her with pleasure.

'Shit-faced scared,' he repeated. 'You really do have a way with words.'

'It's part of my charm,' Maree said through a smile.

'Okay, I've been warned.' Beau laughed again.

'When and where?'

'How is tonight, 7 pm? The concierge at my hotel recommended a restaurant called Becossa ...' He hesitated.

'I'll meet you there,' Maree cut into the silence. She'd had time to think about the logistics of dating a man in a wheelchair.

'Great,' he said, relief in his voice. 'I'll see you tonight.'

'Until tonight.' After she hung up, Maree stood and signaled to her assistant, Allegra, to come help her remove the pinned-up uniform off the extra.

'Who put a smile on your dial?' Allegra asked as she inserted a coat hanger in the police uniform and hung it on the metal clothes rack.

'That was Beau,' Maree said.

'So he did call.' Allegra wheeled the clothes rack into the corner, making sure to avoid a dressmaker dummy encased in a taffeta Civil War-era gown. 'I guess better late than never.'

'He's shy,' Maree said.

'Ah-ha.' Allegra walked over to her desk and sat on the edge. 'Just the way you like them.'

'Do I hear judgment?' Maree asked, detecting an undertone in Allegra's voice.

'I'm just wondering what's his thang?' Allegra carefully arranged her long skirt around her legs as if she was posing for a photo shoot. Allegra was a lover of vintage fashion and treated every day like it was a dress up day. Today she was wearing a black and white, pin-striped 1950s dress, and stockings with a seam running down the back of her legs. 'Since you only take on self-help projects.'

'I do not,' Maree said.

'Really?' Allegra frowned at her. 'What about the single daddy and his five little kidlets?'

'That wasn't a pity thing. Andrew was sweet and kind.' Maree remembered her last boyfriend. They'd met at the supermarket when his youngest daughter, a two-year-old toddler, attached herself to Maree's legs. Andrew had come running a few minutes later, apologizing profusely, while calling out to his ten-year-old son to stop using the trolley as a skateboard.

Maree's heart had melted as she saw Andrew's stress as he tried to track his children all over the supermarket. She'd left her trolley in the aisle and helped him with his shopping, and found out he'd become a single father after his wife passed away from cancer six months before.

'Andrew was using you as a nanny,' Allegra said.

'He needed help,' Maree countered. It was true that Andrew had needed quite a lot of help so that he could catch up on work, and in the three months that they were an item Maree ended up spending a great deal of time with his kids. But she hadn't minded. She'd fallen in love with them.

'Anyway I love spending time with his kids.' Even after they realized that their relationship was lacking the passion that should have existed, they'd become firm friends and Maree still regularly babysat his children.

'Yes, you love spending time with them more than with their daddy, which says it all.' Allegra waved her hands, her neon nails shimmering. 'And let's not forget the one before that. Darren the entrepreneur.'

'David,' Maree corrected. She'd met David at a launch party, one of those affairs that others might view as a golden ticket but she only saw as a work function. A mutual friend introduced her and David and they'd hit it off. He was charming and passionate, and soon they'd drifted into a relationship.

'He needed a profile and you became his private product placement consultant,' Allegra said.

David had a great idea to make jewelry out of recycled products. Maree believed in his dream and she'd recommended him to her costume designer friends, who used his jewelry when designing outfits for their characters. Within a year he'd moved from developing prototypes to receiving orders from luxury jewelry stores.

'His company is doing great now and I'm receiving income on the shares,' Maree said.

'Yes, but you're not the one warming his bed,' Allegra reminded her. 'Last time I saw him in the society pages he was wrapped like an anaconda around a Victoria's Secret model.'

'Things didn't work out,' Maree said. 'It happens.'

When David's company took off he'd become busy and a relationship was too hard to juggle. They'd soon come to the mutual decision that while the spark was there, their timing was off.

'We're still friends though.' They'd just been to lunch a few days before.

'And that's another problem,' Allegra said. 'You can't be friends with all your exes. It's just not natural.'

'Says the woman who ritually burns her exes' belongings,' Maree said.

Allegra was known as High Maintenance. She was always attached. In the two years Maree had known her, the longest Allegra had ever gone between relationships was a month, and that was because she was bedridden with the flu.

And Allegra's relationships never lasted because of her hair-trigger temper. The minute her boyfriends stepped out of line, taking too long to call back, or eyeballing a waitress who served them, there was hell to pay. Her temper tantrums rivaled tsunamis because of the destruction they left in their wake. She treated men like disposable accessories and always assumed there was something better around the corner. And she was usually right. With her almost cartoon-like hourglass figure, striking face and lush lips, men were never in short supply.

'Enough digressing. You haven't answered my question. What's wrong with this guy?' Allegra demanded.

'Nothing.' Maree leaned over her desk pretending to flick through her sketchbook, her long hair hiding her flushed cheeks.

'Fess up,' Allegra demanded. 'I know there's something wrong. Your whole body language is screaming guilt.'

Maree hunched further, desperately turning pages of her book. Allegra tore the sketchbook out of her hands.

'Tell me now or I'm going to torpedo your desk.' Allegra tossed the book on the floor.

'All right, all right,' Maree gave in, knowing that this was no idle threat. Her desk was always artfully littered with sketches and pieces of material. If Allegra followed through she'd never be able to find anything. 'He's in a wheelchair,' she muttered as she bent to pick up her sketchbook off the floor.

'What was that?' Allegra leaned closer.

'He's in a wheelchair.' Maree sat on her stool. She waited for Allegra to launch into a tirade, but instead silence greeted her. She looked up and found Allegra staring at her with pity. 'What?'

'I blame that father of yours for making you think you're not worthy of anything better.' Allegra shook her head sadly.

Maree felt anger take hold. 'I'm getting coffee.' She grabbed her bag and headed for the door. She never could deal with confrontations. Her throat got choked up and she couldn't force any words out. Escape was her only option.

As she stalked out of the building and onto the studio lot, she felt shaken up by Allegra's reaction. By the time she'd completed the ten-minute walk to the coffee bar on the lot, her anger had eased and she was melancholy.

She hated being the object of pity. As she waited for her coffee among the tourists completing the studio tour, she wondered how much truth there was in Allegra's statement. So she liked men who were vulnerable and gentle. What was wrong with that?

She noticed a guy checking her out in line. He was breathtakingly handsome, impeccably dressed, and his hair was perfectly styled—a dead giveaway that he was an actor. There was something familiar about him. She'd probably seen him on a poster somewhere.

Maree sensed he was building up to speak to her, and she quickly moved away, turning her back to him. She hated guys like that, who looked like they had just stepped out of a Vogue magazine. She was drawn to men who were real and unaffected by vanity.

Her order was called and Maree stepped up to the counter. She could see Mr. Vogue eyeing her, probably viewing her disinterest as a challenge. She was relieved to get out of the café. She heard someone calling to her. She turned over her shoulder and saw Mr. Vogue pursuing her. She gave a sigh of frustration. She should have known he'd be the persistent type.

He caught up to her and said hello. Maree tried to shake him off, but he asked her out anyway, only to receive the stock-standard answer she gave to all actors—a firm and resounding no. She only dated men who weren't associated with the entertainment industry.

Maree took the scenic route back to her office, passing by the wrought-iron entrance gates. She sipped her coffee as she walked through the studio lot and remembered the movies she'd watched being filmed behind each door as a child.

Her parents met on the set of *The Valiant and the Vain* on which they were both stars. After a whirlwind wedding, they had an even quicker divorce when Maree was only one year old, and her mother realized that her father's on-screen persona as a womanizer was a case of art imitating life.

When she was eight years old her mother passed away and she went to live with her father, which meant the studio became her second home. She'd spent her childhood and adolescence traversing every building on the forty acre lot and became well known to the grounds and security staff, which ensured she was able to finagle her way into many movie sound stages.

She was eleven years old when she snuck onto the first *Mission: Impossible* set and watched Tom Cruise perform that iconic and much imitated stunt of hanging from a harness above a white floor. When she saw the movie at the cinema, she had her first taste of understanding the make-believe world of movie-making. With its mix of tin sheds and large buildings, the studio lot might look intimidating to most people, but to Maree it was almost as familiar as the palm of her hand.

As she walked along slowly, her thoughts returned to Beau, and she wondered if Allegra was right. Was she only going out with him because of pity? She remembered the way that his feelings seemed to be written on his face. No, Allegra was wrong. Maree was definitely attracted to him and she knew he was attracted to her. She just wanted the opportunity to see whether he lived up to her expectations.

Maree had never cared about a man's assets or looks; her only requirement of a potential partner was a good heart. Growing up in the business, she'd been around beautiful people all her life and knew that their good looks were just a quirk of genetics. Others might idolize movie stars and anoint them as chosen ones, but Maree knew that beauty was most times skin deep, and led those endowed with it to believe they were owed something from the world.

Seeing her father in action her whole life she had decided early on that she would never date an actor, that she wanted a man who was genuine.

When she returned to her office she placed Allegra's skim macchiato on her desk.

'Seriously, Maree, I'm the one who should be giving a peace offering,' Allegra said as she lifted the cup to take a sip.

'I know you're just looking out for me.' Maree hung up her bag.

'Yes, I am,' Allegra said. 'But it doesn't mean I have to be a bitch about it. I've been thinking about your date.'

Maree knew from Allegra's wicked smile that it was going to be something she wouldn't like hearing.

'There are perks to dating a man in a wheelchair,' Allegra said coyly. 'A little cunnilingus goes a long way.'

'Oh, God.' Maree burst into laughter. Her stomach hurt by the time she finished.

'Just remember that I want to hear all the dirty details.' Allegra twirled in her chair.

'There will be no dirty details,' Maree said.

Allegra lifted her eyebrow, indicating her disbelief.

Maree shook her head and tried to get back to work, but she kept remembering the shape of Beau's mouth. She flushed as she wondered what his beard would feel like against her skin.

Chapter 3

Tom was paying for his purchases when his phone rang. He'd gone to a shopping mall so he could find the kind of wardrobe that would suit Beau.

'Where are you?' Carter demanded as soon as he answered. Tom could hear the tension in his voice.

'Shopping,' he said.

'You need to get to the studio now,' Carter shot out. 'Ryan Green is meeting with Ken Grey.'

Tom's hand tightened on the phone. Ryan Green was a bankable star whose profile was bigger than Tom's. He was meeting with Ken Grey, the director of *Heroes of Tennessee*, the movie that Tom was putting everything on the line for, including living part-time as a man in a wheelchair.

'But we've got a contract.' He'd felt such a sense of pride and relief as he'd signed his name with a flourish on the dotted line.

'Not finalised yet,' Carter snapped. 'Meet me at Prime Studio. I'll be waiting by the gates.'

Tom wanted to demand answers, but Carter had already hung up. He'd signed the contract a month ago and had assumed the counter signatures were completed and the contract just had to be forwarded by Carter's office to him. Now he was finding out that his dream part could be just that, a dream.

He debated about calling back, but decided the best course of action was to get to the studio. Carter probably had some plan to stop this disaster in its tracks and Tom just had to trust that it would work.

As he drove to the studio he remembered Maree worked at Prime. He hoped he wouldn't bump into her. He didn't want her to meet 'Tom' on the same day she had her date with 'Beau'. It was too risky. In the end he decided he was worrying unnecessarily. After all it was a forty acre studio lot. What were the chances they would bump each other?

After he parked his car he walked toward the gate and saw Carter, red-faced and beginning to sweat under the warm sun.

'Let's go,' Carter said, talking quickly and walking even more quickly as he led Tom down a street of the studio lot. 'Wendy was meeting Ken for lunch and I want to head her off.' Tom read between the lines. Carter had spies all over the studios; usually they were waitresses or ushers who were aspiring actors and happy to do favors for one of Hollywood's top agents. Carter was hoping to bump into Wendy and feel her out about the movie. Wendy was Marketing Director of Marco. She was also married to Ken Grey, the director of *Heroes of Tennessee*. Carter had worked out an arrangement whereby Tom agreed to be the face of Marco, if Tom got the part he wanted. Ken had held off on signing the contract, and now he was in meetings with Ryan Green, the actor that was rumored to be his first choice all along. But Wendy had as much to lose as they did if Tom didn't get the part.

'There she is.' Carter nodded at the platinum blonde unlocking a Mercedes. 'Wendy,' he called, walking towards her with his arms held out.

Wendy looked up. Seeing them bearing in her direction, her face took on a pained expression and Tom's heart sank. This didn't look good.

'Carter and Tom.' Wendy trilled with laughter as she accepted Carter's kiss on the cheek gracefully.

Tom nodded, carefully keeping a distance between them. He knew how to play this part of the game.

'I'm so glad we bumped into you,' Carter said.

Wendy looked sceptical that this meeting was accidental.

'Tom and I were just talking about the Marco campaign,' Carter said.

'I sent you a signed copy of the Marco contract yesterday,' Wendy said with a tight smile.

'Of course you did,' Carter said. He shot Tom a quick look.

Tom could feel his scalp tightening with anger. He should have suspected a double cross. Ken had been dragging his feet on the film contract, tweaking clauses for the past two weeks so that they were tied down to Marco, but leaving Ken in the clear to drop their agreement and sign on another actor for *Heroes of Tennessee*. Ryan Green had been unavailable due to a scheduling conflict, until three weeks ago when a tsunami hit the tropical island that was the setting for his movie shoot, canceling it indefinitely.

'We were just meeting with Peter Barton,' Carter continued. 'He wants Tom to be the lead in Marlon.'

Wendy frowned. Marlon was a biopic of Marlon Brando and required the lead actor to age in order to play the life story, including putting on huge amounts of weight for the latter years.

'Of course Tom wasn't able to do it because he was committed to *Heroes of Tennessee*, but if that were to fall through ...'

Carter let Wendy connect the dots. Tom saw the horror on Wendy's face as she realized that an obese Tom Calvert would not give her the marketing edge she'd been hoping for.

'Anyway, say hi to Ken for me,' Carter said, a bright smile on his face.

Tom stepped in beside Carter and walked back to the parking lot.

'I'll be expecting Ken to call me within the hour to smooth over our misunderstanding,' Carter added smugly.

Tom nodded. He should have been happy, after all *Heroes of Tennessee* was supposed to be the role that would change his life, but instead he felt dispirited. He was sick of Hollywood machinations and never being able to trust anyone. It was like walking through a jungle and never knowing when he would step into quicksand. God knows he had thought about quitting, especially after the scandal that nearly derailed his career.

Two years ago he'd been arrested at a nightclub with cocaine in his possession. It wasn't his cocaine. He'd been helping a friend dispose of it, but the arrest had fed a long-held rumor in the tabloids about his drug addiction and his career had taken a hit.

Then, a year ago, when he'd gotten what Carter dubbed 'the Hollywood seal of approval' in the form of his very own obsessive stalker, his childhood dream of becoming an actor fast became a nightmare. While living as Beau was about guaranteeing his future so that he could make the kind of movies that mattered to him, it also gave him a breather to be incognito some of the time and avoid his stalker for a few months. He just had to hope that his life would change after *Heroes of Tennessee* was released.

'Buck up.' Carter clapped him on the shoulder. Tom shrugged despondently. 'Let's get a coffee before we hit the traffic again.' Carter led them through the studio maze to a café. As Tom followed him inside, he looked up to see Maree standing in line. He froze. He should leave before she saw him, but his feet didn't move. He wanted to see what would happen if she did see him. She must have sensed she was being watched, because she looked up again as she stirred sugar into her coffee. Tom didn't know what he expected. Usually when women realized he was interested, they smiled and engaged. Maree gave him a once-over and turned away. He kept watching her, waiting, sure this was a ploy and she was playing it cool. She glanced at him again, her face creasing in annoyance before she mingled with the crowd so she was hidden from him.

'Here.' Carter returned and gave him his coffee. He started talking, but Tom wasn't listening. He was scanning the crowd for Maree when he spotted her leaving the café.

'Just hang on for a moment,' Tom said, and turned to follow her. He stepped out onto the street behind her. 'Excuse me,' he called. He didn't know what he was going to say, but he couldn't stop himself.

She glanced over her shoulder but kept walking.

Tom ran and caught up to her. 'Hi,' he said, catching her eye as he fell into step beside her.

'No.' Maree sped up.

'You don't even know the question.' Tom laughed despite himself.

'I don't need to,' Maree said. 'It's always going to be no.'

Tom was thrown. This was not how he'd imagined the conversation to go.

She was walking away and he only had a second to come up with a way of stopping her.

'Even if I told you I've got tickets to the Oliver Stone premiere.' He blurted out the first thing that came to mind, and flashed his best movie-star smile. 'Everyone who's anybody will be there.'

'Not everyone,' she said, matter-of-factly.

Her voice had an edge and Tom realized that she wasn't playing a flirtation game with him. She really didn't want to go out with him.

'Please.' Tom lifted his hands in a pleading gesture. 'I didn't mean to offend you.'

'When?' she asked. 'When you implied that I'm a celebrity chaser, or that I'm a nobody?'

'I'm sorry,' Tom said, honestly perplexed. This wasn't the Maree he'd met yesterday. This Maree was prickly and standoffish, with none of the softness he'd encountered then. There was an awkward silence as he tried to decide how to extract himself.

'I've actually got plans tonight,' she said, taking pity on him. There was a look in her eye. The kind of look that a woman gets when she's thinking about a man she's attracted to.

'He's a lucky guy,' he said.

Maree smiled and he finally recognized the woman he'd met. 'I'm a lucky girl.'

'Maybe in another life I might have met you first,' he said.

She hesitated, as if she was thinking through how to answer.

'You don't think so?' he asked, pushing her. She shook her head softly.

'Ouch.' He grabbed hold of his chest. 'You're tough on my ego.' She laughed as she waved over her shoulder.

He watched her walk away with regret. Getting to know Maree had started out as a game. A way of guaranteeing he was more genuine in his part. But now the game was changing. It wasn't about being Beau anymore. Maree had his attention in a way that no other girl did. He couldn't wait for their date tonight.

'So I guess you scored,' Carter said when he returned to the café.

'No, I didn't.'

'Really?' Carter gave him a bemused look.

'Actually I'm not the lucky one.' Tom sipped his coffee. 'Beau has a date with her tonight.'

'What?' Carter raised his voice. 'Is that wise?'

'It's all part of my research,' Tom said.

'And what if you don't pull it off and your date goes to the tabloids? I didn't spend months organising the biggest movie deal of your career to have it fall apart because of one date.'

Tom felt momentarily guilty. Carter had put his career on the line to make *Heroes of Tennessee* happen. He'd known that Ken Grey wouldn't consider Tom Calvert, former soap star, for the part. It was Carter who suggested that he transform himself into Beau and audition in character. And it had worked. Tom got the part, but one of the clauses of the contract stipulated that no one was to know Tom Calvert was attached to the project. He had to be in character for the whole two months of the shoot, and his casting would only be revealed at the premiere.

'You need to cancel,' Carter said.

Tom's stomach dropped. 'Why?'

'Because you can't do the deed as Beau. Your legs work. They will twitch, you will move. It will be immediately obvious that you're not a paraplegic, and that will raise questions you don't want to have to answer.'

'So,' Tom said. 'It's not as if I'm going to have sex on the first date.'

Carter quirked an eyebrow. That was usually Tom's M.O.

'Beau is different,' Tom insisted. 'The rules are different for him. He wouldn't expect to score on a first date.'

'Okay, but don't say I didn't warn you against this.' Carter looked at his watch. 'I've got to get back to the office. Call me tomorrow and update me on your date.'

'Will do.' Tom threw away his coffee cup in the bin and got in his car. He had a lot of preparation before him.

Chapter 4

Tom arrived at Becossa, a romantic restaurant that he'd enjoyed on many previous dates, and pulled up at the entrance. He was driving a new vehicle, a MV-1, which had special hand controls that allowed those in a wheelchair to drive. It was purchased for the movie *Heroes of Tennessee* and Carter had arranged for Tom to borrow it.

When the valet saw the modified car approach, he directed Tom to the handicapped parking space at the rear of the restaurant. Tom picked a suitable car space that had extra space on the right side of the car.

He lifted himself across to the passenger side where his wheelchair was secured, then manoeuvred the chair back to the side door and pressed a switch that activated a ramp. He gently wheeled down onto the asphalt. After activating the switch for the ramp to retract, he closed the side door.

As he wheeled himself around to the restaurant entrance, he realized that for the first time in a long time he was filled with trepidation at a first date. Before he called Maree, he'd debated long and hard about the logistics. In his other life he would pick her up in his flashy sports car, opening and closing the passenger door for her like a gentleman.

In this life he had no such option. If he did pick up Maree, he would have had to ask her to sit in the backseat as there was no passenger seat, and she would have had to watch the process of him getting in and out. In the end he'd had to accept that the simplest and least awkward option was to meet at the restaurant.

As he wheeled himself up the ramp beside the stairs to the entrance he was bemused by his own complacence. Since being in a wheelchair he felt like he'd been half blind before, oblivious to the world of the disabled. He'd been in and out of this restaurant on numerous occasions yet had never noticed the wheelchair ramp.

The waiter showed him to his table, and as he wheeled himself onto the patio he became aware of the reaction Beau was receiving. As Tom Calvert he was used to being watched after all his years in the public eye, but since he sat in the wheelchair he was more self-conscious.

When he was ushered to his table he was relieved to see they'd followed the instructions he'd provided when making a reservation and there was only one chair. He maneuvered himself to the empty side, the white tablecloth draping over his wheelchair and hiding it from view.

The restaurant was an outdoor patio with a huge ancient tree in the center, its gnarled branches curving into the sky and over the heads of the diners. Lit by candles, there was an intimate ambience and Tom felt his discomfort fading. No one would be able to clearly tell the difference between the back of his wheelchair and the restaurant chairs.

As he waited for Maree to arrive his nervousness returned. He'd had to leave much earlier than he usually did to ensure everything went smoothly for his first date as Beau, and now he had nearly half an hour of waiting stretching out in front of him. He'd never had to wait for a date before; if anything he was the one who always arrived slightly late, knowing that the women waiting for him would gladly wait for Tom Calvert.

Now that he was on the receiving end, he realized how arrogant he'd been. In this vacuum of time there was opportunity for self-doubt to creep in. He was questioning his choices, from his decision to wear black slacks and a navy and white striped shirt he'd bought for Beau, sans tie, to tying his hair into a ponytail in order to appear more presentable. By the time seven o'clock came around he was regretting asking Maree out, calling himself a fool for plunging into this method acting gambit, and ruing the day the *Heroes of Tennessee* script had landed in his lap.

He'd felt a surge of excitement when he met Beau Tennant on the page and realized that this was the part that could change his life. Up until this moment he'd considered that day his date with destiny, now he was wondering if it was a trick that Hermes, the Greek God of trickery, had been playing on him instead.

When he saw Maree walking behind the waiter at three minutes past seven, all his nerves evaporated. She took his breath away. She wore a powder blue dress that highlighted her delicate waist and curved over her cleavage. Her waist-length hair was tamed into a side ponytail that bounced as she walked toward him. She was beautiful, but in a natural, girl-next-door way. She didn't look fake and manufactured like some of the starlets he'd dated.

He tried to stand to greet her and remembered himself as his hands gripped the arms of the wheelchair. Instead, Maree leaned down and kissed him on the cheek. He breathed in her scent and felt her silky hair brush against his cheek. A slow burn of desire started low in his stomach.

'You look beautiful,' he said, his throat catching.

'Thanks,' she said. 'You look pretty nice yourself.'

He rubbed his chin. He'd trimmed his scruffy beard and tied his hair up after slicking it back. He'd had to be careful not to make himself look too much like Tom and highlight his facial features.

'I'm feeling such a strange sense of déjà vu,' she said after the waiter had seated her.

He stilled. He knew he shouldn't have approached her earlier today. Now she'd seen him as both Beau and Tom in the same day and he could inadvertently give himself away.

'It's probably the restaurant,' Tom said. 'You've been here before?'

Maree nodded. 'That's probably it.'

As her face cleared he felt relief settle on him.

'This is for you.' He handed her the white carnation he'd bought her. Usually he arrived to a date armed with roses, but when he'd been in the flower shop earlier that had seemed like a cliché and he wanted this date to be special in every way.

'Thank you.' She took the flower and breathed in its scent. 'It's beautiful.'

The waiter returned with the champagne he'd requested to be served when his date arrived.

'That's an expensive bottle,' Maree said after the waiter took their orders and left. 'Are you sure you can afford it?'

He realized that Beau Tennant, former war veteran, shouldn't have that much disposable income. 'My friend and I sold the screenplay so I'm celebrating.'

'Congratulations.' Her tone held a question mark.

'Don't say it,' Tom pre-empted her. 'I know once the movie is made I'll lose all privacy, but the movie may or may not happen. It's Hollywood after all.'

'You're learning.' Maree laughed. 'There is no certainty in this town. Except that everything is uncertain of course.'

'You sound pretty negative about your hometown,' Tom said. 'I felt like that about my home and that's why I left.'

He was in safe territory here. Beau and Tom both came from Tennessee, that's why he felt like the part was written for him. He'd known boys like Beau all this life. He'd grown up around them. He'd even aped them in high school, pretending to be one of the jocks, while inside every single atom longed to be part of the glee club. But he'd been too afraid to step out of the high school hierarchy and be true to himself.

Tom had gotten into college and then quit within the first semester. Tired of trying to be something that he wasn't, he'd finally decided to pursue his acting dream, despite his parents' dire objections that he'd end up a bum. He'd jumped on a bus and hightailed it to Los Angeles.

Beau's story was similar. He'd left his hometown, jumping on a bus and hightailing it, but he didn't have Tom's academic achievements to bolster him, or his acting ambition. So he'd signed up with the army in an effort to escape his mundane existence. Beau thought he was being a patriot and saving his country, and he'd ended up in a wheelchair for his naivety.

'So why haven't you left your hometown?' Tom asked.

'I planned to,' Maree said. 'I went to college in New York to try to get away from the film business; I wanted to get into costume design on Broadway. I soon realized movie making was where I wanted to be. When my godmother, Antoinette, was retiring as costume designer on *The Time of Our Lives* she put in a good word for me and I got the job. I kind of fell into things a bit, but I've been working on developing my portfolio, and I'm getting some work in movies.' She smiled wryly as she held the glass to her face. 'A few indie flicks. I did the *Fairytale Princess* costume.'

'I saw that,' Tom said. 'I remember that scene when she jumps off the cliff in that flowing dress.'

'That was my dress.' Maree gripped his hand. 'I designed it and worked with the art director to make it look cinematic.'

'It's an image that really sticks with you.'

'That's what I want to do. Create those iconic movie moments, the ones that stay with you and become part of your memory bank.'

The waiter returned to serve their dinner.

Maree picked up a mussel. 'There's a producer who's interested in working with me on his next film, so keep your fingers crossed.'

'Tell me about the movie,' Tom asked, cutting into his pork chop.

He recognized the plot as one he'd been offered and turned down because he didn't want to do back-to-back movies. It was a post-apocalyptic blockbuster and there was much scope for a whole new dimension with costumes. As he watched Maree talk, the lights bringing out the copper in her hair, her brown eyes sparkling with joy, he felt something he hadn't felt for a long time: the stirrings of infatuation. Since he came to Hollywood he'd only felt lust for other women. Some of them had been challenges to be conquered, others were the result of loneliness and needing a connection. A few affairs had lasted months, but as soon as his lovers started wanting more, Tom would cut ties. His whole life was consumed by his career and, until he was able to achieve his goal of becoming a serious actor, he couldn't focus on a relationship.

'I'm excited for you.' He lifted his glass. 'Here's to our dreams coming true.' While Maree was talking, he'd recognized the same yearning he had to make his dream reality. He'd had to fight to stay in character and remember he was Beau.

'What about you? What's your dream?' Maree asked.

For a moment he was about to answer as Tom. 'My dream has changed now,' he said finally.

'Because you ended up in the wheelchair,' Maree said.

'Yeah.' Tom smoothed his hand over his hair. He kept trying to remember he was in character, but he just felt like he was lying. 'I'm working on something at the moment, but I don't want to say too much and jinx it.'

'Fair enough,' Maree said. 'Been there. I thought I was on a definite run with a movie, and then at the last minute the director decided to employ his latest paramour, so I missed out. Three months of my life went down the toilet. Now I like to wait until things are set in stone before I get excited.'

'To taking our time.' Tom raised his glass again.

Maree accepted his toast. 'To being able to share our dreams soon.'

He lost himself in her eyes. There was such hope and light he saw there. It broke through his jaded persona and he wanted to see the world through her eyes again.

Tom cleared his throat. 'I watched *The Time of Our Lives* and admired the Civil War costumes Penelope and Brad wore,' he said, 'Your work?' One of the current storylines featured a reincarnation storyline during the Civil War.

Maree smiled delightedly. 'I'm flattered. Not many of my dates confess to watching a soap opera.'

'It's one of the advantages of being a tourist. I'm free during the day.'

'Tell me more about the movie?' she asked.

Tom rubbed the back of his neck, feeling rattled. He hadn't thought this through. Telling her he'd sold his screenplay was a cover, and he hadn't considered the consequences.

'It's about my experiences in the war and how I got injured,' he said reluctantly. The more he talked, the more there was a chance he would give too much away.

'If you're having trouble telling me about it, then you really should re-think making a movie.' Maree finished her glass. 'Once the movie is out there you're going to have every Tom and Harry poking their nose into your business and demanding more.'

'You sound like you're talking from experience.' Tom poured her more champagne. The more comfortable she got, the more the pressure was off him.

'My first mistake was Larry Tenner.' Maree twirled her hair around her finger as she stared past his shoulder. 'He was my boyfriend and I thought he liked me. I was wrong.' Her mouth formed into a smile that didn't reach her eyes. 'His main goal was meeting my dad so he could score an audition. That's how he got his first walk-on part.' She sipped her champagne.

'That's horrible,' Tom said.

'It is, but it's things like this you need to be aware of.' There was pain in her eyes. 'These are the people that come out of the woodwork when you have something to show for yourself.'

He wanted to reach over and take her in his arms. He knew too well the pain of learning that someone you considered a friend only wanted to use you. He tried to think of a way to help her feel better, but he was tongue-tied. An uncomfortable silence descended.

'Wow, I really know how to ruin a date.' Maree's face flushed and she put her hands on her cheeks.

'No, no.' This was his fault. He'd wanted her to drink more in order to loosen up, but instead he'd stumbled upon a painful topic. *Well done, Calvert,* he cursed himself. Tom reached across and took her hand. 'I've been there.' He spoke slowly, thinking through his words. Maybe there was a way he could share his story without breaking his cover.

Maree was looking at the table, still embarrassed after her outburst.

'His name was Kane and I thought he was my friend. We grew up together, but I enlisted in the army while Kane went to college. After he graduated, Kane enlisted too, and was given the rank of Specialist. I'd just been promoted to Corporal. Even though we were both receiving the same salary, a Corporal is considered a commissioned officer and has leadership respon-sibility, while a Specialist does not.'

He felt relief when Maree met his eyes again.

The words were coming easier as he cobbled together his story using his acting coach's advice of melding truth with fic-tion. Kane was his roommate when he first came to LA. They'd shared an apartment for the three years that Tom was modeling and doing extras work while he tried to sign with an agent. When Tom signed with Carter and scored his first break getting a part on a soap, the two of them went together to all the Hollywood parties that Tom was suddenly invited to. He was twenty-three years old with his first taste of success, and he and Kane sampled everything together—the women, the booze, the party drugs. Eventually Tom arranged for Carter to take Kane on as a client. He was sure that his friend's big break was just around the corner, but Kane was impatient.

'I thought we were buddies who always had each other's backs, but Kane didn't see it that way. He was resentful that I was his superior officer.'

Maree was the one holding his hand now, giving him comfort as he opened himself up. He hated remembering this and acknowledging how naive he'd been. Tom took a sip of water, buying himself time as he remembered the last part of his story.

Tom got Kane a walk-on part on the soap, and that's when he discovered his friend's true nature. After a particularly heavy night of debauchery, Kane lied to him about his call time the next morning. When Tom turned up on set three hours late, he'd found that his supposed good friend had told the director he was a drug user.

The director was ready to fire him, and it was only Carter's intervention that saved his job. Even so, Tom had to take a urine test that showed up positive, of course, so he had to do a short stint in rehab in order to keep his job. Kane hadn't gotten him fired, but he did succeed in almost ruining his career. After this, Tom became a tabloid target as the Hollywood bad boy—a stain on his career that he'd been trying to eradicate ever since.

He put the glass down and continued Beau's version of the story. 'We were on rec leave and Kane turned back my watch so I was three hours late signing back into the unit. The Corporal was all ready to write me up when one of my other buddies lied and said he'd played a prank on me by turning my watch back, not realizing I would be late.'

After the pain of his friend's betrayal, Tom got his former roommate out of his life, and had made sure that all his new connections remained acquaintances and nothing more.

'I'm sorry,' Maree said.

He cleared his throat. He'd never told anybody about Kane. He'd been too ashamed, but telling Maree had brought to surface the pain of his friend's betrayal.

'As you can see someone doesn't have to be an actor to do bad things.' Tom removed his hand from hers under the pretext of reaching for his glass, but he just needed time to recover from the emotional aftermath.

'Maybe,' Maree said. 'But in my experience they're more likely to.'

Tom felt the sting as her words hit home.

'So if I was an actor I wouldn't be on this date with you?' he asked with a smile.

'No,' Maree said flatly. She waved her hand like she was shooing a fly. 'I don't date actors.'

'Ever broken the rule?'

'Never have, never will.' Her voice brooked no argument.

'Okay.' Tom felt slightly perturbed.

·♥·♥·♥·♥·♥·

By the time they finished their dessert he was firmly back in character, and had pushed Tom out of his head. Beau started to tell her funny stories from his army days. 'And that's how I found out how Snake got his nickname,' Tom said finishing his latest story, and watching with delight as Maree laughed.

The waiter returned and handed him the bill holder. Tom opened it and removed the receipt and the credit card. He'd borrowed Carter's card in order to ensure his anonymity.

Tom gestured for Maree to lead the way and he wheeled his chair behind her. He admired the view from where he was, but was frustrated that he couldn't walk beside her, draw his arm around the deep curve of her waist and feel her body against his. His hands itched to touch her. He'd give anything to be able to kiss her, but that seemed like an impossible dream.

Chapter 5

Maree reached the entrance and handed her keys to the valet. She turned and looked down at Beau. Her breath caught at the undisguised desire in his eyes. Her attraction to him had been building all night. There had been a moment when she had gotten too tipsy and revealed too much of herself, but instead of being a disaster, it had led to them having a real moment of connection.

Sitting across from him it had been easy to forget the wheelchair and enjoy the man. And she had. She loved his wit, the drawling Southern accent that made her tingle whenever he said her name, and had found herself glancing at his lips. She could see no way of gracefully maneuvering a kiss in the entrance of the restaurant.

'I had a wonderful night.' She bent to kiss him on the cheek.

Beau turned his head at the last moment and their lips touched gently. She went to straighten, feeling exposed in the open restaurant entrance, but he placed his arm around her waist and pulled her down onto his lap.

'Beau,' she said his name in shock.

'Shh.' He wheeled them down the side of the building while she held on with her arms around his neck. He stopped the wheelchair and looked at her. 'I'm going to kiss you now.'

His face was in shadow, but she could hear the need in his voice and it made her gasp. For the first time since they'd met she had to look up at him and she felt a thrill as she realized how broad and strong his shoulders were.

He bent his head and placed his lips against hers. He gently pressed on them, urging that she open his mouth to him. She did and he brushed his lips against hers. His beard tickled her face, but soon she forgot everything as he gripped her tightly, his lips devouring her until she struggled to breathe. Her head was leaning back on his arm, while her hands kneaded at the hard muscles of his chest.

Beau lifted his lips off hers and they both panted for breath, taken by surprise at the strength of their passion. Maree hadn't felt this sort of infatuation since she was in high school, and she felt slightly panicky. Like she was stepping out on a ledge. The men she'd been with had been safe, the thrill of attraction had been missing. She'd always kept herself slightly aloof in relationships. She didn't want to lose herself completely, and being with Beau set off warning bells. He made her feel so vulnerable.

But there was also something about the look in his eyes that made her feel like they were kindred spirits. When he told her about his betrayal she realized how much they had in common. He too found it hard to trust people.

She put her hand on his cheek and as their eyes met, there was a moment when she knew he felt the portent of what was to come. She was sinking into him, her initial attraction developing into something more, something deep and real.

Part of her wanted to run away, right here and right now. Just get up and run for her life, because she knew that this man was going to change her world forever. But another part was desperate to know where they were heading, thrilled at the possibility of finally finding someone. Maree had given up on love; that melt-your-bones, all-consuming love. She'd thought that there was something wrong with her; that having her father keep her at a distance and losing her mother when she was too young had broken something inside her; that because of this she was never able to feel what other women described.

She'd felt stirrings like this only once before, with the boy who'd used her in high school, and the trauma of his betrayal had stung so deep she'd never allowed herself to feel like that again. But now she was feeling it with Beau and it made her realize that maybe she wasn't broken. Maybe what Allegra had been telling her all along was true and she had just needed to find the right man.

Maybe she finally had? Beau was the real deal. He wasn't involved in the business so she didn't have to worry about secret motives. What you saw was what you got. He was a straight up and down guy who exuded honesty.

'I wish ...' He stopped.

'What do you wish?' she asked.

'I wish I could see you again.'

'That can easily be arranged.'

'I'll call you tomorrow,' he whispered as he brushed his lips against her cheek.

'Tomorrow.'

She gripped his bicep as she lifted herself up. 'You're very strong.'

He smiled. 'There are perks to being a wheelchair.' He turned the wheels and she walked beside him.

Desire filled her as she imagined all the things they could do with his strength.

When they returned to the restaurant entrance the valet was waiting with her keys. Beau watched her as she got in the car. She met his eyes from the driver's seat, and felt a thrill at the intensity of his gaze. He waved as she drove away. She couldn't wait to see him again.

·♥·♥·♥·♥·♥·

The next morning she walked into work with a smile on her face.

'I can see your date went well. Spill.' Allegra perched on Maree's desk.

'Nothing to tell. It was a lovely date and he was a gentleman.' Maree put her handbag in the bottom drawer of her desk.

'That's all you're going to give me,' Allegra demanded. 'After all the details I give you after my dates.'

'You don't think I actually enjoy hearing all that, do you?' Maree asked with a deadpan face.

Allegra looked dumbstruck. 'Nice try, but I'm not letting you off the hook.'

Maree sighed as she looked down, her hair hiding her face. She didn't want to talk about her date last night. It all felt so precious and she just wanted to hug the memories to herself and re-live them in her own time. She was scared that if she talked about it she would jinx what was developing between them.

'Don't tell me you're falling for him?' Allegra pushed her hair out of the way so she could see Maree's face. 'Oh, no. It was only one date.'

'But what a date,' Maree sighed. 'I have never felt so comfortable and connected with another man.'

'Okay, maybe he is special and what you have is real,' Allegra said as she gripped Maree's hand. 'But just make sure you know what you're getting yourself into. Give it some time and really get to know him before jumping in with both feet.'

Maree smiled tightly and nodded. She knew that Allegra was just looking out for her, but she resented the fact that reality was already intruding on her feelings for Beau. She just wanted to be in the romantic bubble and enjoy the moment without having to keep her guard up.

When her cell phone rang an hour later she smiled when she saw Beau's name on the screen.

'Hello,' she said.

'I thought I would try waiting to call, but I couldn't.'

Maree glanced at the time. It was twelve o'clock. 'I'm glad.' It was nice to be with someone who didn't play games.

'Would you like to have dinner tomorrow tonight?' he asked.

According to dating protocol she should check her diary and not be too eager. 'I would love to,' she said without hesitation.

'Great. I'll text you the address.'

After they hung up Maree sat in her chair and smiled. While she always loved her job, today it felt especially easy because she was floating on a cloud of happiness. She started working on her sketches and as usual time flew by.

Her phone beeped that she'd received a text. It was from Beau. She turned her chair so she could read it in privacy.

'I'm sitting where we first had coffee and thinking of you.'

Maree felt a flush of joy sweep over her as she read his words.

'Hopefully nice thoughts.'

'Not so nice. I keep remembering how you looked the other night. You took my breath away.'

Maree hugged the phone to her chest, wanting to squeal like a teenager. She loved that he was thinking of her and sending her messages, rather than playing the dating game of waiting a certain amount of time to touch base. She sent him another text.

'You looked pretty wonderful yourself. What are your plans for today?'

'Doing some sightseeing, but will be back in my hotel room to watch my favorite show at 1 pm.'

Maree laughed with delight. That's when *The Time of our Lives* began. Allegra gave her a curious look. Maree got up and went to the stock room and wedged herself among the colorful tubes of material.

'That's an interesting choice of daytime television.'

His text quickly followed. 'I'm hoping to get some design inspiration from the characters' wardrobe. Have a big date tomorrow night and want to impress.'

'I don't think you need to try too hard.'

'Maree,' Allegra came to the door. 'They're here.'

She nodded. The actors that were booked for their costume fittings had arrived.

'I have to go, work calls.'

Maree returned to her desk and put her phone in her handbag, just in time to see Beau's goodbye text.

'I'm guessing that was your Southern Beau,' Allegra teased.

Maree smiled without saying anything.

'Well, I'm impressed. You've already graduated to naughty texts.'

'They're not naughty,' Maree said. 'They're nice texts.'

'Ah, ha,' Allegra said.

Maree shook her head, annoyed she was falling for Allegra's bait. Soon she settled into the rhythm of the day, coordinating fittings and alterations for outfits, but there was a constant undercurrent of anticipation. She was looking forward to her date with Beau and seeing him again. Whenever she thought about him she felt butterflies in her stomach.

Maree was eating a baguette at her desk for lunch. Allegra had stepped out for coffee and she was alone. She looked at the clock. It was 1.15 pm. She had a devilish thought and reached for her cell. 'Are you enjoying today's episode?'

'Not really. Brad just died.' He punctuated with a sad face.

She smiled. There was something so reassuring in knowing that he was the type of person who did what he said he would. It was a quality that she cherished after her experiences with celebrity chasers and hangers-on. 'Don't worry, everything will turn out for the best.'

'Okay, I'm trusting you. I'll keep watching.'

'Keep the tissues ready.' She found the live feed on the internet and watched the episode. She waited a few minutes and sure enough there was another text message.

'What! Penelope dies too? This is too much.'

This was her favorite episode. She'd had to be on set to manage the wardrobe for the Civil War re-enactment on a sound stage with a faux Southern mansion. She'd watched the filming of the scene when the two star-crossed lovers, Brad and Penelope, were supposed to have their happy ending, only to die tragically in each other's arms.

Brad was a Union soldier and Penelope a Southern belle. They fell in love when he was ordered to garrison her home as a makeshift hospital. Brad was smuggling Penelope out on a hospital convoy while she was disguised as a nurse, but a jealous rival betrayed them. Brad was shot when he threw himself in front of a bullet for Penelope.

As she held her dying lover, Penelope leaned down and kissed him on the lips. 'We will be together forevermore my love,' she whispered. 'Wherever you go, I go.'

As the camera panned out, the wound on her side became visible. The convoy continued while the two lovers lay on the road.

Maree had originally loved the storyline because it gave her the chance to really put her design skills to use. She'd spent months researching the historical period and recreating the costumes, sourcing the material needed and learning to make the outfits.

But watching the final scene, something unexpected had happened. Maree thought she would feel elated at the work she had done and sad that the storyline was ending; instead she'd felt a longing to experience that sort of romance. Even though she was watching two actors mimic a great love, it had reminded her that such emotions did exist in the world and that somehow they had bypassed her. She'd wondered if there was such a thing as soul mates, and whether she would ever get to meet hers.

The camera panned up to the sky, going higher and higher as the two lovers became smaller. Soon they were gone and only sky filled the screen. The camera spiraled, faster and faster, and suddenly stopped. It panned wide again and came down onto the same street, but now there were electricity poles beside it.

The two actors who played Penelope and Brad were back on the street, only now they were wearing contemporary clothing and standing beside two cars that had obviously careened into each other. As the scene continued with the two characters arguing, Maree received another message from Beau.

'True love never dies.'

'Not in Hollywood anyway.'

She suddenly felt frustrated. Why did she let this fake romance make her feel inadequate? Why wasn't it enough to meet someone and fall in love? Why did she buy into this ridiculous notion of a mythical soul mate that then made every romance seem banal?

Beau wrote: 'True love is real. It's just our expectations that are not.'

Maree was intrigued. 'Do tell.'

'Finding love, falling in love, and staying in love is special enough. We don't need to complicate things more with ridiculous notions.'

Maree typed her reply, 'You're speaking my language. I get so frustrated with the ideal of perfect love that we see everywhere.'

'Love is not perfect. My favorite quote is 'Love begins with a smile, grows with a kiss and ends with a tear.' No matter what the journey, the destination is the same.'

Maree felt something shift inside her. She'd always thought of love as salvation, yet now she realized it was just a regular part of life and like everything it would someday end. That's why it was important to cherish it when it came along.

She looked down the phone in wonder. She'd never had such a forthright conversation with a man about relationships or expectations. Usually they just bounded along, dating and figuring things out, until things suddenly didn't work. It made her realize why it felt so special with Beau. She could talk to him about things she had never talked about with anyone else.

'That's a beautiful quote. Thank you for sharing it.'

'You're welcome, Maree.'

Allegra came in, carrying a cup in each hand. Maree felt exposed, almost as if she'd been caught in the act of undressing. Beau had made her lose all sense of time and place. Even though she and Beau weren't physically together, she'd never felt such a sense of intimacy.

Maree returned her phone to her handbag. She worked until late, getting her design sketches ready for the next production meeting. By the time she got home it was 8 pm. She put spaghetti on to boil and went to her bedroom to change into her pajamas. When she returned to the kitchen she took a container of her home-made bolognese sauce from the freezer and defrosted it. Within fifteen minutes she was snuggled on the couch watching The Bachelorette while she ate her dinner.

She received a text during a group date and groaned as she reached for her phone. She should have turned it off. Her annoyance faded when she saw it was Beau.

'Thinking of you.'

'Me too,' she typed, her eyes still on the TV screen.

'Men Today? Is that a secret code I'm missing?'

Maree snorted with laughter as she read the text. She quickly wrote back.

'So sorry. Damn autocorrect. I was watching *The Bachelorette* and wasn't paying attention.'

'Very brave of you to confess to watching that.' He added a winky face emoji.

'I like some trashy television in my down time. Anyway it's not as if you can talk.'

'Touché. I would argue *The Time of Our Lives* is more high-brow compared to *The Bachelorette*.'

'Mmm, I'm starting to suspect that you're not a regular watcher of TTOOL, Beau.'

'Okay, you've got me. I was watching it just to impress you.'

'I already suspected that was the case.' She inserted a smiley face.

'Okay, I'm turning on the television to see what the appeal is.'

They spent the next few minutes sending each other funny text messages as they watched the faux romance play out on the screen.

The next group date was at the zoo. Maree started tensing up when the group entered the reptile enclosure. In the next shot the Bachelorette was experiencing a close encounter with the wildlife and had a white python draped across her shoulders.

Maree screamed and covered her eyes. 'I can't watch,' she typed into her phone. 'You'll have to tell me when it's over.'

'What's the matter?'

'I hate snakes.'

'You know it can't get out of the television.'

'Doesn't matter. I can't look.'

'Really?'

While the segment was on she texted him the story of her first and only camping trip with her father and her step family when she was ten years old. On the first morning she'd just crawled out of her tent when she noticed a stick moving. Looking closer she saw it was a snake. She froze, her whole body shutting down. The snake crawled over her foot and then started wrapping itself around her calf. She was wearing shorts, and the snake's cool, scaly texture made her skin break out in goosebumps, but she couldn't move even if she wanted to.

Her father was by the campfire when he finally noticed what was happening. He rushed over and picked up a stick, using it to prod the snake off her body and throw it away into the bushes. Her stepmother insisted they leave and Maree never went camping again.

'Wow, that's intense,' Beau wrote when she finished. 'No wonder you have a snake phobia.'

'I wouldn't say it was a phobia.'

'And denial is not a river in Egypt.'

Maree laughed. 'Okay, maybe it is a phobia.'

As the credits rolled Maree yawned. 'Time for sleep. I've got a big day tomorrow.'

'Oh. Big plans?'

'Yes, I've got a date with a hot Southern gentlemen.'

'Then you should definitely get some shut eye. Good night.' He sent her kisses.

After Maree brushed her teeth she went to bed, falling asleep with a smile. She couldn't wait until tomorrow's date.

Chapter 6

Tom received a text message from Maree while he was waiting for Carter.

'Hope you're having a good morning,' she wrote.

Great morning, but an even better day because I'm going to be seeing you.'

'Can't wait for tonight.'

'Me too.' He looked up to see Carter approaching. 'Gotta go.'

Tom turned off his phone, feeling slightly perturbed. He'd sent his first message to Maree as an impulse. He'd been sipping coffee as Beau at the café where they met and had thought of her. It had seemed like a harmless flirtation, a way of building anticipation for their date, yet somehow their texts had taken a serious turn.

Carter sat down and ordered his coffee. 'Are you coming over tonight?'

Tom hesitated, drawing a blank.

'The game's on,' Carter prompted.

The cobwebs cleared and Tom remembered they'd made plans to watch the Los Angeles Lakers.

'I'm going to have to pass.' Tom rubbed the back of his neck.

'Why?' Carter demanded.

Tom hesitated. Carter had already expressed his disapproval of him dating Maree, he was not going to be happy when he found out about their second date.

Carter's eyes narrowed. 'Are you going on another date with Maree?'

Tom nodded, taking a sip of his coffee.

'No, absolutely not. You have to cancel.' Carter's voice was definite.

'What's the problem? My disguise is working. There's nothing to worry about.'

'Really. Ever heard of the expression, don't push your luck?' Carter asked.

'What about the one, nothing ventured, nothing gained,' Tom countered.

Carter's face changed and he became amiable. 'Look, what's the big deal? There are beautiful women everywhere who haven't seen you as Beau and Tom. Women who we don't have to worry about breaking your cover.'

Tom knew that what Carter was saying made sense. There was no need for him to only date Maree. In fact if he was thinking about it logically it would be better for him to date other women and truly put his cover to test. He glanced at his phone and remembered their text message exchange. They had only known each other for a short time, yet he had shared with her things he had never told another woman.

Perhaps he needed to heed Carter's warning. Maree was getting under his skin in a way no other woman had. He thought about it for a moment. He thought about picking up the phone and sending her a text message canceling, but something inside him rebeled at the notion. While he knew it would be more logical to cancel and move on, he couldn't do it. He couldn't stop thinking about Maree, remembering the way they'd crossed paths. She intrigued him with her mixture of heart and spunk.

Carter shook his head. 'You're not going to cancel, are you?'

'I can't,' Tom said. 'I have to see this through.'

'Don't tell me you're falling for her!' Carter demanded.

'No, of course not.' Tom pushed aside his misgivings. 'It's just that, she's like my Everest. That peak that I have to climb and truly prove to myself that my cover as Beau is bulletproof. If I can do this as Beau, well, then I can do anything.'

'Okay,' Carter sighed. 'As long as this is only about work.'

Tom nodded.

Carter tapped his fingers on the table. 'Then we need to make sure that your cover truly is bulletproof and the only way to do that is to really make you a paraplegic.'

'Whoa.' Tom held up his hands. 'While I'm all about suffering in the name of my art, I'm not willing to go that far. You're not taking a crowbar to my spine.'

Carter rolled his eyes, but Tom was not reassured. You could never take anything for granted with Carter.

'I was thinking we could call my friend who's a doctor. She might have some advice for how we can make sure that Beau's cover survives all possibilities.'

'What possibilities?' Tom asked. 'I'm not planning on sleeping with her.'

'Yeah, right. A leopard can't change his spots, and all that,' Carter said.

'I'm not. It's not Tom Calvert going on a date. It's Beau Tennant.'

'You might know the difference, but little Tom does not,' Carter said, pointing at his lap.

'I can control myself.'

'Okay, let's just work through this scenario.' Carter leaned forward and lowered his tone. 'You and Maree finish your date. You pull her down on your lap and start giving her a kiss. You're cool and in control. It's just going to be a quick goodnight kiss, but just like that things change. Something about the curve of her neck, the way she's sitting in your lap all sweet and malleable is getting your juices flowing. You lean in for another kiss. You get caught up, just for a moment, and as you do your leg flinches. It moves. Now remember she's on your lap and she can feel everything. Maybe she doesn't notice because she's caught up in the moment too, but maybe she does.'

Tom rubbed his neck. 'All right. Call your doctor friend.'

Carter gave him a grin. 'You've made the right call, my man,' he said, picking up his phone and dialing.

Tom listened as Carter arranged a meeting the same night. He hoped he wouldn't live to regret this.

·❤·❤·❤·❤·❤·

At four o'clock Tom was in his apartment, sitting in his wheelchair as Beau, when Carter walked in with a woman carrying a medical bag.

'This is Dr Diane Collins.' Carter performed the introductions and sat on the sofa.

'We met at Carter's New Year's Eve party a couple of years ago,' Diane said as she sat on an armchair.

'Of course.' Tom nodded. That party was not one of his finest moments. It was just after he'd been arrested and he'd received a rejection that morning for a part he thought he'd had in the bag. By the time he got to Carter's party he was already half drunk and he made sure he stayed that way. The rest of the night was a blur—he only had faint images of a woman he hooked up with, and of noticing her wedding ring afterwards. Loathing had filled him as he realized that he'd broken yet another one of his rules.

'But something tells me you don't remember me,' Diane said, seeing through his paltry attempt at faking it.

'My apologies,' Tom said. 'I was so drunk I barely remembered my own name.'

Diane smiled. 'No need to apologize. It was only a passing introduction. So I understand you have need of my medical services for tonight?'

Tom looked at Carter for help, wondering what he'd told her.

'Diane knows about your performance tonight as Beau, and that you're nervous about breaking character. So she's come up with a solution.'

'That's right,' Diane said. 'I can inject you with a muscle relaxant in your pressure points and it will numb the nerves in your legs.' She opened her bag and began preparing syringes.

Carter blanched and started for the kitchen.

'Is something wrong?' Diane asked.

Carter eyed the syringe with horror. 'Those things give me the heebie-jeebies.'

After he left, Tom and Diane exchanged a smile. 'So are you ready?'

He nodded and Diane went to stand behind him. 'Lift up your shirt.'

Tom hesitated. He didn't need to do this to be more believable as Beau. He'd already got the part and he was getting practice every day just by being in the wheelchair. He pictured Maree's face and felt a surge of anticipation. She'd been so helpful and kind to Beau, yet so abrasive to Tom. He'd never had the experience of a woman preferring a regular Joe Blow to a movie star. She was a puzzle he wanted to solve, and the only way he could see her again was if he went on a date with her as Beau. He lifted his shirt and felt a pinprick in his lower back.

'Is this performance open to the public?' Diane asked, returning the used syringe to a disposable container.

'No.' Tom shook his head. 'It's more of a private affair.'

'Really?' Diane picked up another syringe and waited.

'I'm sort of auditioning for a producer,' Tom said, feeling he was under obligation to explain.

Diane nodded. 'Roll up your jeans, please?' She administered a few more injections.

Within minutes he felt a numbing sensation and soon he couldn't feel anything at all. For the first time Tom really felt what it was like to be paralyzed and it was terrifying. He tried to imagine his whole life stretching out in front of him without being able to walk and fear opened up in his stomach. He just wanted to stand, to be able to move his muscles. His head started spinning and sweat coated him.

He pinched his legs. 'I can't feel anything.' Panic clawed at him.

'It's only temporary.' Diane patted his arm. 'It will last for eight to twelve hours.'

Tom took a hold of himself. There was nothing to worry about. This was a treatment people had every day, he reassured himself.

'Can I drive?' Tom asked as Diane returned her paraphernalia to her bag. 'I have a handicapped-modified car.'

'I don't see why not,' Diane said. 'It's not as if you're using your feet.'

Tom nodded. He used hand controls and his arms were unaffected. His mind was clear and the only effect of the injections was the numbness in his lower body.

She looked him up and down. 'No one would believe that Tom Calvert was under there.'

Tom felt more confident after her assessment, but there was something in her tone that made him wary.

'What a lucky girl she is to inspire all this,' Diane said and left the room.

As he looked at himself in the mirror he had to agree, no one would guess that he was wearing a disguise. He wondered why he wasn't reassured by that thought. Diane's tone sounded as though she was judging him for playing this deception on Maree. Remembering Maree's generosity of spirit he felt a nudge of guilt, but quickly pushed it aside. It was one date. What could possibly go wrong?

·♥·♥·♥·♥·♥·

As Maree walked into the restaurant, she felt butterflies flutter in her stomach. She couldn't believe that she was so nervous about her second date with Beau. After their text messages she felt like the stakes were higher. While she'd liked him, now there was this feeling that they were headed somewhere, and she hoped that Beau felt the same.

She had a glimpse of him sitting at the table before he noticed that she had arrived and her heart filled with tenderness. He turned his head as if he'd sensed her presence and their eyes caught. She'd always thought that the romantic cliché of time standing still was just a fiction, but as they gazed at each other, the sound of metal cutlery hitting china and the hushed conversations of other diners disappeared until all she could hear was the sound of her heart.

She started across the room, her black silk dress swishing as she walked. He watched her, his eyes filled with desire. When she got closer she saw something more, something she hadn't seen in a man's eyes, but she didn't recognize it. She leaned down and kissed him on the cheek, feeling a flutter as they touched.

The waiter seated her and as he told them the specials, Beau reached out and held her hand.

'How was the rest of your day?' she asked after the waiter had left with their drinks orders.

'Really long,' Beau said.

'Mine too.' She laughed, delighted with his honesty. Usually she arrived at work and it felt like she blinked only to find the day over, but today time had seemed to move in a strangely lethargic fashion. She'd found herself looking at her watch so often that Allegra had noticed and teased her about it.

She asked him about the tourist spots he'd seen so far and this led to her reminiscing about what it was like growing up in Los Angeles, while he told her about growing up in Tennessee. Even though their upbringing couldn't have been more dissimilar, they even joked that he was a little country and she was a little rock 'n' roll, they had both spent most of their childhoods feeling lonely and like an outsider. They both came from blended families and he'd had a stepfather and she a stepmother and half siblings who made them feel like they were cuckoo birds that had hijacked a nest.

Before she knew it they were having coffee and dessert, signaling that their date was over. After Beau had paid they left together.

'I'll walk you to your car,' Beau said.

As they walked through the parking lot together her skin tingled in anticipation.

'Thank you for a lovely night,' she said, when she reached her car.

Beau took her hand and pulled her onto his lap. He tilted her chin up and kissed her. She realized she'd been waiting all night for this. During their first kiss she'd been surprised by the strength of their passion, but this time she was surprised by Beau's tenderness. His kiss was slow and tender, as if he was savoring the moment.

A car alarm beeped, the sound breaking through their passion. A couple was getting into the car next to them. Maree went to stand up, but Beau held her waist.

'Not yet,' he said. 'I need you to provide some cover.'

She laughed. 'Gives new meaning to the words body shield.'

They giggled like two teenagers, caught up in their pleasure of each other. She'd never been silly with someone like this before.

'Well that answers one question,' she said wryly as Beau placed his hand under her buttocks and lifted her slightly to ease the pressure on his erection. She'd spent the past two days wondering about him, Allegra's teasing about cunnilingus igniting a maelstrom of questions about Beau's abilities.

Beau burst out laughing, hiding his face in her hair as hysterics shook him. She smiled, loving the feeling of his chest vibrating against hers.

'I've never dated a woman with such an earthy sense of humor,' he said.

'And that's not even my best feature,' she quipped and got up. She pressed her key to unlock her car and looked at Beau.

He was looking at her with a strange expression on his face. 'Is something wrong?'

'I just realized I've never met anyone like you.'

'You say that like it's a bad thing.'

He shook his head and smiled. 'Of course not. I'm just surprised, that's all.'

'Good.' Maree opened her car door. 'So would you like to follow me home to make sure I get there okay?' she asked.

She'd been wondering all day about how would they progress their date to the next level considering that they were arriving in two different cars, but it was Allegra who had provided the solution while teasing her.

'I would love to,' Beau said. 'But I can't.'

'Okay, then.' Maree sat in the car and opened her window. 'I'll see you tomorrow.'

Beau nodded.

She turned on the car and was about to start reversing when he called her name.

'I'm really glad I met you.'

'Me too,' Maree said. She held his gaze, not wanting to leave.

Beau moved his wheelchair away. She saw him in her side mirror as she drove away, watching her, and felt a flutter in her chest. She was already missing him.

Maree was about to turn onto Hollywood Freeway when her phone rang. She quickly clipped in her Bluetooth and pressed it on. Her stomach tingled as she waited to hear Beau's voice.

'Maree, it's Mack-Attack,' a deep male voice said in her ear.

Her face drew into a frown. 'Are you okay?' Mack only called when he needed something. Most times his requests for favors involved Maree bailing him out of jail.

'Need to see you,' Mack said. 'Come to me.'

Mack had an aversion to talking on the phone. He didn't consider the line safe.

'Okay,' Maree said.

'You'll find me in the usual—' The phone cut out.

Maree breathed a sigh of frustration. She reached the interchange on to Hollywood Freeway and debated a moment, her fingers tapping on the dashboard. If she turned right she would be heading home to Sherman Oaks and she'd be asleep in her own bed within the hour. If she turned left she'd be going downtown to see Mack. As much as she wanted to go home, she couldn't resist Mack's call for help. With a sigh she turned left and headed to Skid Row, the fifty square block where the Los Angeles homeless population slept at night. Skid Row had the distinction of having the highest concentration of homeless in the United States.

During the day this area of downtown was the fashion and toy district and was lit up with color from wholesalers displaying their wares. At night the colorful fabric and plastic wrapped toys were hidden away inside, leaving the sidewalks free for homeless people to come and sleep on a patch of cardboard, or pitch a tent, or wheel their shopping trolleys full of their belongings.

There were plans underway to build permanent housing for the homeless, but as Maree drove down San Julian Street and saw people setting up their sleeping quarters, she realized how slow change was in coming.

Mack was waiting for her at his corner. She rolled down the window as she pulled up to the curb beside him.

'Hey.' He peered in and saw her dress. 'I hope I didn't take you away from a date.'

'I was on my way home,' Maree said wryly. Mack was not known for his patience and if he'd called during her date, she would have had to leave. 'What do you need?'

'I want you to meet someone.' Mack opened her door.

Maree took her handbag and keys and stepped out of the car.

'Bring your coat,' he said.

Maree looked at him and lifted her eyebrow. She hadn't brought a coat. It wasn't like she'd been planning to drive into LA's most notorious neighbourhood, nicknamed The Devil's Den by some residents.

Mack heaved a sigh as he took off his army coat, and placed it around her shoulders. Even though it was well worn, it was clean and the smell of laundry detergent filled her nostrils.

Mack led her to a tent a few feet away from them. 'Hank,' he called and waited.

A head peered out. Hank saw Maree and his head quickly disappeared back into the tent. A few moments later he emerged, tugging on his cap.

'This is the friend I was telling you about,' Mack said.

Hank looked at Maree like he couldn't believe she was there. She expected him to reach out and pinch her at any moment.

'Maree, this is Hank. He worked as a forklift operator until a month ago when he was laid off,' Mack said.

Maree held out her hand. 'Nice to meet you, Hank.'

Hank reached out and gently shook her hand.

'Dad, can I come out, too?' A little boy was peering out of the tent, watching them.

'Not now, son,' Hank said. 'I'll be a moment.'

'Hank and his wife and two kids were evicted from their condominium when they couldn't pay rent anymore,' Mack continued. 'I thought maybe you could put in a good word for him with the maintenance crew at your studio.'

Maree gave Mack a sharp look. 'I'll see what I can do,' she said. 'I'll call with any news.'

Hank nodded, his eyes tearing up. 'I can't believe it.' He took off his cap and squeezed it between his hands. 'I thought your fella here was just talking to fill the time when he said he'd get me off the street within a week. I didn't actually believe he'd do it.'

'Well, Mack has a way of making things happen.'

'Thank you.' Hank squeezed her hand one more time.

Maree nodded, and Mack led her away.

'You could have given me some warning,' Maree snapped under her breath when they were out of earshot.

Mack gave her a blank look.

'What if I can't get him a job?' she demanded, feeling the responsibility for Hank's family on her shoulders.

'You will. You can do anything when you're motivated enough.'

'You don't know that.' Mack's unwavering belief in her abilities was like a stone around her neck. 'What if I fail them?' She shrugged off Mack's jacket and threw it at him. She was unlocking her car door when Mack took her arm.

'You're upset,' he said.

'Yes.' She knew she shouldn't get upset with him; he couldn't help the way he saw the world, but she felt so overwhelmed. Mack was like a bull doing the Pamplona run. All he saw was the chase, he didn't notice the details.

Maree tugged her arm away to wipe the tears collecting in her eyes. She didn't realize that she was standing so close to the edge of the pavement and her right heel slipped off and broke, sending her flying backwards.

Mack's arm shot forward and he grabbed her shoulder, pulling her back onto the sidewalk and ripping her dress in the process.

Maree heard a shout and turned to see Beau wheeling himself quickly toward her.

'Hey, leave her alone.' Beau shouted. 'Get behind me, Maree.' He wheeled himself around in front of her, forcing Mack to step away or risk his feet being rolled over.

'What do we have here?' Mack asked.

Maree saw the half smile under his beard.

'Beau, it's okay.' She put her hands on his tense shoulders, standing awkwardly as she balanced herself on one heel. 'This is my friend, Mack.'

'Friend?' Beau repeated.

'Is that what we are?' Mack asked.

'Yes.' Maree wanted to slap him. It was just like Mack to show his sense of humor at the worst possible time.

Suddenly Mack's eyes sharpened as he looked over her shoulder. 'Get her out of here,' he said to Beau and hurried toward a group of youths who were harassing a man lying in a doorway across the street.

Beau scanned the street. 'Follow me.'

Maree saw his car was parked behind hers. She followed, limping along with her broken heel, when Beau suddenly stopped.

'Come here,' Beau said gruffly, pulling her onto his lap.

'You don't have to.' Maree hugged him. She could feel the muscles in his arms moving as he pushed the rim wheels to turn them.

The ramp was still mounted from his car. Maree hopped off his lap. 'Thanks for the ride,' she said and walked up the ramp ahead of him. She sat on the backseat and waited as he retracted the ramp and closed the door.

Maree's mouth was dry as she faced him. Beau was so take charge in this moment that she realized this was why she was attracted to him. Despite his vulnerability, he was also strong.

'Are you okay?' Beau asked, misunderstanding her silence.

Maree nodded. 'How did you find me?'

'I was following to make sure you got home safely,' Beau said. 'Who's Mack?'

Maree looked away, not keen to revisit that part of her history. 'Mack was a high school friend,' she said, skirting the edges of truth.

While she and Mack had gone to the same high school, their history was much deeper than that. She'd known Mack most of her life. His father was the director on *The Vain and the Valiant* and his mother took over as leading lady when Maree's mother died. They were two kids who spent way too much time on the set, unattended and bored because their parents were busy with their careers.

'You've come to a place like this, at this time of the night, for an old friend from high school?' Beau asked.

'He needed me.'

'And you came running.' Beau's voice was full of disbelief. 'Is he more than a friend?'

'No, of course not,' Maree said. 'We were latch-key kids whose parents were always too busy, so we found our own entertainment. We drifted into a bad crowd and developed all the usual vices that came with the LA party scene.'

Whenever she remembered those days she felt a knot in her stomach. She had been unconcerned with anything but getting the next hit and remaining in her drug-induced world where she didn't feel lonely and unloved. There was always a party and another guy whose attention would fill the void for a few hours. After a few drinks Maree didn't care who he was, she just wanted the affection that came with intimacy.

'One night I was driving us to a party after we were already loaded, and we crashed.' She clenched her hands in her lap.

Beau reached over and took her hand in his, comforting her as he listened to her story.

Her date had been in the passenger seat and Mack was in the back with a girl he'd met the night before. Before they got in the car they had all taken some party drugs, and Mack had gone to a drugstore to get them alcohol, using his fake ID. Maree was sipping from the bottle when she turned the wheel too hard, sliding off the road and down a ravine. When the car came to a stop, her date was unconscious from hitting the windshield.

After the police breathalyzed her, she was arrested and charged with driving under the influence. She spent the night in lock-up, waiting for her father to come and bail her out. In the morning she was told she had a visitor. She expected her father, but when she arrived in the visiting room it was Mack waiting for her.

'He's not coming,' Mack said. 'Our parents are only interested in how our addiction affects their reputations, they're not interested in us.'

It was the first time she suspected that all her experiments and vices were a call for help. They were a way of trying to get her father to notice her. When she looked into Mack's eyes she saw his betrayal and anger and realized that he was telling the truth, something broke inside her.

'I'm bailing you out.' Mack placed his hand on the glass. 'They're processing the paperwork and I'll be waiting for you outside.'

Maree forced a smile as she put her hand on the other side of the glass.

'I'll get you through this,' he'd promised.

And he did. She'd received a court order to undertake rehab and Mack had voluntarily admitted himself so he could support her. During counseling she'd come to terms with her feelings for her father, and began to accept that he would never be the father that she wanted.

When they got out of rehab three months later, Mack was the one who encouraged Maree to follow her dream and go to New York, while he followed his dream to travel the world. He'd popped into her life over the years, somehow always knowing when she needed him most. The last time she saw him was two years ago when Antoinette died.

Maree had started to think something terrible had happened to him, when she found him by accident a year ago. Whenever costumes had passed their use by date, they were donated to a shelter, and Maree had been dropping them off when she saw Mack leaving. He'd ignored her when she called out his name and it was only because she chased him down the street and threw herself in front of him, that he'd finally stopped. He looked so different—a beard covered his face, there were lines under his eyes and on his forehead, making him look much older than twenty-eight—but it had only taken Maree one look into his eyes for her to know that it was her childhood best friend.

'Gerald Mackevoy is dead,' he'd told her. 'I'm Mack.'

He was sparing with the details about the past ten years of his life. All Maree knew was that Mack didn't want anyone to know who he really was, and that he had become a champion of the downtrodden.

Since then she'd only seen him a handful of times, and whenever she did it was always to help his cause in some way, but she didn't mind.

'He's lucky to have you as a friend,' Beau said, looking at her with admiration.

'I'm lucky to have him as a friend. Don't look at me like I'm a saint.' It made her uncomfortable. 'I'm a former druggie.'

Beau pushed her hair away from her face. 'You made a bad choice, but you didn't let that define you.'

'The only reason I'm here is because of Mack.'

Mack had saved her life; he had known she didn't have the strength to see rehab through by herself. Because of him she got clean and never went back to the life of partying and one night stands. And she wasn't ever going to forget she owed him.

'You are one loyal woman.' Beau said it as if it was a quality he hadn't come across often.

'Yes, I am.' She met his eyes. This was one truth she knew about herself. Once she accepted someone, they always remained a part of her life. She knew what it was like to be abandoned and discarded.

'I wish I'd met you before,' he whispered, as he leaned across.

'No.' She cupped his face. 'I don't care that you're in a wheelchair. All I care about is you.'

He blinked, and pressed his forehead against hers. She didn't want him to put her on a pedestal. She'd had enough boyfriends that saw her as the 'perfect girlfriend' who fulfilled their needs. The reason she loved being with Beau was that he saw her as a woman with her own desires and needs.

She kissed him. He gave in to her, pulling her onto his lap and holding her tight as if he wanted them to merge together into one. Maree felt a restlessness inside and she wanted to wrap herself around him. It was Beau who stopped first.

There was a bang on the window and Maree turned. Mack was standing outside the car.

Beau pressed the button for the window, and it slid down.

'You can go now,' Mack said. 'They've moved on.'

Maree saw that the youths behind him were walking away down the street. Somehow Mack had managed to defuse their hostility.

Beau pressed open the door. 'I'll follow you home,' he said.

'You don't have to,' Maree protested.

'Yes I do.'

Maree saw the determination in his eyes. She realized that he was feeling the same thing she did. Somewhere along the way, they'd crossed a line and merged with each other. Maree nodded and smiled at him. She felt him watching her as she walked to her car, holding onto Mack's arm for balance.

Chapter 7

As Tom drove behind Maree after their date, he'd tried to identify the feeling that was burning in his chest. He'd started this whole adventure as a way of changing his life and gaining some much needed time away from the mess he'd made of it. When he first met Maree, he'd been attracted to her, but his primary objective was to use her as an opportunity to rehearse. Sometime during their date tonight he realized he was falling for her, but he'd still tried to keep his guard up and remain in disguise—until they kissed. That kiss made him realize that he was fooling himself. She was under his skin and there was nothing he could do about it. He'd realized that he had to re-think this whole romance.

He'd waited in the parking lot as she drove away, but there had been a bottleneck on the road outside the restaurant and he found himself driving behind her. He decided to follow her home and make sure she was all right. When she'd taken a right turn and headed into the city rather than home, Tom had been confused. He'd realized that she wasn't going home after all and he didn't want to spy on her, but he became concerned when she'd entered Skid Row.

When he saw her with Mack he'd been convinced she was in danger, and his protective instincts had asserted themselves. He was glad that Carter had insisted on making his disguise foolproof before he left, otherwise he would have leaped out of the wheelchair to rescue her.

When she told him about Mack and her father, Tom realized his instincts about her had been right all along. She was the real deal. She was sweet and loyal and kind. He'd seen the emotion in her eyes as she looked at him, and he knew she was falling for Beau. She didn't care about the wheelchair or the trappings of success. She really only cared about what was in someone's heart.

He felt the size of a gnat. Maree had shown him nothing but kindness and generosity and all he'd done was lie to her. There was a feeling in his gut that he almost didn't recognize—he felt guilty at the way he'd treated her. She deserved someone who cherished her for who she was, not someone like him who was only out to use her.

He pulled up in Maree's driveway and watched as she exited the car. He knew what he had to do. He couldn't see her again. That was the only way to make this right.

Maree came to his window, still hobbling on one heel. 'Did you want to come inside?'

'No,' Tom said brusquely. 'I'd better get home.'

'Oh.' Maree was taken aback by his curt tone. 'So I'll talk to you tomorrow?'

He couldn't leave her with the hope that he would call. He turned toward the windshield. 'I think it's best if we don't see each other again.'

'What changed?' she asked.

'Nothing.' His hands clenched on the steering wheel as he forced the words out. 'I've just realized that it's probably best if we nip this in the bud now. There's no future for us.'

'But I don't care about the wheelchair. I just care about you.' She reached in through the window and placed her hand over his.

'Don't.' He took his hand away.

'It's because of me, isn't it?' she asked.

He turned to her in surprise.

'It's because you know about my past.' She covered her face with her hands and stumbled back from the car.

'No, no, it's not,' Tom said.

She started walking toward her front door, her shoulders shaking as she sobbed. The smart thing to do was to let her believe that was the reason. All he had to do was start the car and leave. He put the key in the ignition, and groaned. He couldn't do it. He couldn't leave her believing that he was rejecting her because she was a former drug addict. He knew better than anyone the way that sort of rejection bit into your soul.

'Maree, wait,' he called through the window. She didn't hear him. She couldn't see where she was stepping through her tears and she stumbled, falling onto the driveway.

He quickly transferred into his wheelchair and activated the ramp. He flew down the ramp and up her driveway.

'Maree, are you all right?' he asked as he approached her.

She looked up at him and his heart broke to see the devastation in her eyes.

'Please, Maree, let me help you.' He reached down and helped her up. As soon as she was standing she shook off his hand. 'Can we talk?'

Maree walked toward her front door.

'I want to explain.' He followed her.

She stopped at her front door, keys in hand. 'I think I'd like to hear that explanation.' She unlocked the door without looking at him. She stepped in and turned on the light. After he'd passed by and was inside she said, 'Wait here. I'll be right back.'

As he waited for her to return he felt a nervous flutter in his stomach. He wheeled himself next to the couch and waited. What was he going to say? He needed her to know that he couldn't be with her, but he needed to do it in such a way that she wouldn't be hurt. He didn't know if there was an answer to his conundrum.

He had fallen for her, hook, line and sinker. He put his hand to his chest; he felt a clawing sensation in his heart at the thought of not seeing her again. If she was feeling the same way he was, she would be devastated.

Anger filled him. What the fuck had he done? It had taken thirty-two years for him to find someone he could love, and the most amazing thing was she had feelings for him as well—not for the carefully crafted movie persona, or for his money, but for who he was inside. Yet because of this stupid charade, he had ensured he could never be with her.

Whatever he did at this point, he was going to lose her.

He didn't realize he was crying until he felt a tear drop onto his hand. He touched his cheeks, feeling the rivulets under his fingertips. He couldn't remember the last time he'd cried, yet after two days with Maree she was in his heart in a way that no one else ever had been.

He looked up and saw her in the doorway. She'd changed out of her dress and was wearing a pink T-shirt and sweatpants that clung to her body. Her face was bare of makeup and her eyes were swollen.

'You're crying.' She came and kneeled in front of him. Her arms wrapped around his neck and he leaned down, his head touching hers as his arms embraced her.

'I'm sorry. I'm so sorry,' he whispered against her hair. 'I don't want to hurt you.'

'Then don't.'

They looked into each other's eyes and he felt it again—the sense that this was where he was supposed to be; that his whole life had been leading up to this moment, this woman. She felt it too. He didn't know who leaned in first, but suddenly her lips were on his. His hands cupped her cheeks and he kissed her like she was his oxygen and he couldn't breathe without her.

Tom hesitated. In his mind he had a moment of strength—he did the noble thing and drew away apologetically, before wheeling away from her forever, not ruining her life with his presence. But his arms had a mind of their own. He held her tighter, not able to let go. Even if this was all he had with her, this one moment, he had to take it. He needed to be with her just once.

He gripped her under the arms and pulled her onto the chair, her knees either side of him. Her lips were sweet and her kiss sensual. As they kissed he realized that things were different. Because of the pressure point injections he had no sensation and so for the first time he was in the moment like never before. Usually at this point he would have moved on the proceedings and he and his lover would be naked and in bed; instead they were still fully dressed and he was content just to kiss her until he'd had his fill.

They kissed for what felt like hours, her chest pressed against his so he could feel her every breath. His hand rested on her neck, and he could feel her pulse racing. She tipped her head back. Her eyes were soft and dreamy, her hair mussed and her whole body limp. She had never looked so beautiful than in this moment. His heart filled with a tenderness he'd never felt before.

How could it be that this perfect night, when he finally met the right woman, was also the saddest night of his life? He wanted to savor the moment, savor her. His lips made their way down her chin, to her neck. He pulled her top aside and kissed her shoulder, her arm. She lifted her arms up and he took off her top. He cupped her breasts in his hands and kissed them, before his mouth covered her nipple. Her head fell back as she enjoyed his ministrations.

'Your turn,' she said, when he lifted his head. She unbuttoned his shirt and threw it off. He lifted his arms and she took off the T-shirt underneath. As she dropped his T-shirt on the floor she leaned forward, her breasts pressed against the skin on his chest. He gasped at the sensation of skin on skin contact.

After he put his arms down she bracketed her fingers around his wrists and slowly moved her fingers down, stroking the skin on his arms. She gave special attention to his biceps. While he'd always kept in shape, the past week living as Beau had built up his pecs even more.

He held himself still. His instinct was to reach for her, but he wanted things to be different. He'd never had a woman touch him this way. Her fingers and hands stroked him like he was precious and cherished.

'Where's your bedroom?' he asked.

Maree got up and led him down the hallway. When they reached her bedroom he pulled her onto his lap. Her face was flushed with desire and she was biting her lips to contain herself. His hands danced down her navel and he pressed on her clitoris with his thumb. She moaned and he felt a kick of excitement. He'd never been so in control. He put his fingers into her panties. She was damp and slick.

He lifted her off his lap and onto the bed. He took off her tracksuit, and panties. Maree was completely limp and pliable. He wanted to give her pleasure like never before. He pulled her by the knees until he could lower his face to her navel and kiss his way down her stomach. He gently stroked her with his tongue, while his fingers searched her folds and inserted inside.

Maree moaned and lay back. She clenched her hands on the bedding and he loved hearing her moans of pleasure. It didn't take long for the climax to sweep over her and for her to lie dazed and replete. He continued pleasuring her. Her thighs clenched and her hand found his, holding on tightly.

'Please, please,' she begged, her head tossing on the bed.

He lifted himself onto the bed and sat with his back against the headboard. Maree straddled him and undid his pants. His erection sprang free. The muscle relaxant was beginning to wear off and he was feeling an echo of desire rushing through him. He moaned as she lowered herself onto him. He pressed his mouth against her neck, his teeth nipping her flesh, as his hands gripped her buttocks and she rode him. She climaxed and he followed.

Afterwards, they lay together on the bed. Her head was on his shoulder and he felt her soft breath on his skin. She fell asleep, her hand falling from his shoulder onto his chest. He covered them with the duvet, and lay with her for at least an hour, reveling in the sensation of her skin against his. He had never felt so at peace. He didn't want to let her go and have this moment end. Once he left, he wouldn't be able to see her again. This was all he had.

His leg muscles began twitching as the injection wore off. He had to leave before she woke. He laid her head on the pillow, covering her. She stirred, beginning to wake up. He caressed her hair and she stilled, falling asleep again.

He picked up his T-shirt and shirt and dressed, then wheeled himself to the kitchen and found a notepad and paper. This was all he could give her. Some closure from Beau.

As he wheeled himself out of her front door he felt like there was a weight on his chest, making it hard to breathe. So this was what it felt like to have your heart break.

Chapter 8

Maree awoke alone in her bed feeling divine. 'Beau,' she called out, but silence echoed back. He must have left while she was sleeping. She wasn't concerned. She knew he would return.

She walked to her bathroom, her whole body feeling languorous and worshipped from Beau's lovemaking. As she showered she replayed images of their night together. She'd felt such a sense of belonging when they made love. They fit together like they were soul mates.

She felt so happy and alive, as if every moment of her life had been leading up to this. There had been such pain in his eyes when he'd declared his feelings. He'd learned that life was hard and horrible things happened. She would teach him to trust that good things could happen, too.

She stepped out of the shower, and after drying herself, she put on her dressing gown. She walked into the kitchen and started the coffeemaker. When she turned to the fridge and saw the note held up by a magnet, a smile broke out on her face. He'd left her a note.

She leaned forward and read it.

'I'm not a soldier. I'm not a hero. I'm a liar.

I wish I had a met you in another life and was smart enough to recognize a good thing.

I don't deserve you.

I'm sorry for hurting you.'

It took her a moment for the message to sink in. He'd lied to her. He wasn't a solider at all. Numbness washed over her. It was like her body was protecting her from processing what she'd just read. She had to re-read his note, saying the words aloud before she truly understood what he was telling her.

If he wasn't a solider, how did he end up in the wheelchair? Who cares, Maree, he's a liar, her subconscious told her.

He'd told her that he was falling for her. He was probably lying about that too. But she couldn't bring herself to believe it. She had felt a tenderness in his every touch, seen it in his eyes when he'd looked at her. There was something there.

Now she understood the remorse in his eyes and his fear that he would hurt her. He'd told her a lie about why he was in the wheelchair and then he'd found himself unable to confess because he feared losing her. That's why he'd been crying last night.

She knew she should feel angry, but all she felt was empathy. She had to stop him from doing this. He was scared that she couldn't forgive him. She had to tell him that she didn't care how or why he was in a wheelchair. All she cared about was him.

She found her cell phone and rang him. A recording announced that the phone was out of service. She hung up, touching the phone to her lips as she racked her brain for a clue about where to find him. She didn't know the name of the hotel where he was staying. She went to her computer and searched for all the hotels in Los Angeles, doggedly calling them one by one and asking whether Beau had been a guest.

After each phone call her desperation built. She felt like there was a clock ticking down minutes and if she didn't find him soon, she never would. He would return back to his home in Tennessee and permanently disappear from her life. By the time she'd gone through all the motels it was lunchtime. She hadn't had breakfast, but adrenalin was fueling her.

She got dressed and drove to the city. She pounded the pavement as she visited the last places where she'd seen him, desperately hoping for a glimpse of him. She searched for him until nightfall and returned home, dispirited and wan. She'd been checking her voicemail every five minutes, but there were no calls. She couldn't sleep that night, racked with grief.

On Monday Maree returned to work at seven o'clock in the morning, sick of tossing and turning in her bed and desperate for a distraction.

'How did your date go?' Allegra asked when she walked in at nine o'clock carrying coffee. Seeing Maree's red eyes and pale color, she became concerned. 'What happened?' She handed Maree her coffee and sat next to her.

'He left,' Maree said, and the tears that were just below the surface started again.

'But you knew he was going to return home.'

'No.' Maree shook her head. She took the note that she'd spent all day yesterday staring at, trying to decode some hidden meaning in the loops of his writing.

'What a bastard!' Allegra said after she'd read it. 'What sort of a sicko lies about being a war veteran?'

'He's not like that.' Maree took the note back before Allegra crumpled it. 'He's sweet and gentle,' she whispered, tearing up again.

'But he left.'

'He didn't want to,' Maree said. 'I know he didn't.'

'Do you really believe that?'

She nodded. 'I know there was something there between us, but he was too scared I'd reject him once he told me the truth. I don't care. I just want him back.'

'But if he lied to you about this, who knows what else he lied about?' Allegra asked.

Maree turned away. She'd had the same question herself in the middle of the night, but then she kept remembering the way he'd made love to her.

'I know that sometimes you think I'm naive,' Maree said. 'But the one thing I do know is that there was something real between us. He felt it as much as I did. If he truly was a liar he could have just left, but he told the truth because he wanted me to know why he was leaving.'

Allegra reached out for the note again. Maree held her breath as she re-read it.

'I guess you're right,' Allegra admitted carefully. 'If he truly was a bastard he wouldn't have left a confession. So did you talk to him?'

'I tried. His phone is out of service. I wanted to see him, but I don't know where he was staying.'

'It sounds like he's gone back home,' Allegra said.

Maree teared up again. That's what she'd thought.

'Don't worry, we'll find him,' Allegra said, giving her a pat on the shoulder. 'It shouldn't be that hard.' She opened her laptop and typed his name into the search engine and began clicking on links.

Maree watched over her shoulder, breathless with excitement. The phone rang and Maree answered, struggling to concentrate as she kept glancing at Allegra's screen.

'I'll keep looking throughout the day,' Allegra told her when she hung up. 'You concentrate on work. You have to get the designs ready for the production meeting.'

Maree reluctantly nodded. 'Thank you,' she whispered as she squeezed Allegra's arm in passing.

Allegra smiled. 'You know I'm very good at finding men,' she said, wrenching a smile from Maree.

Maree spent the whole production meeting glancing at the clock and tapping her foot, eager to return to Allegra and see what she'd found. She had to fight to concentrate and answer questions when they were directed to her.

'Any luck?' she asked Allegra, striding back into the office.

'Some,' Allegra said, swiveling the screen around so Maree could see. 'These are all the Beaus I've found.'

Maree scrolled through the list. 'None of them are him.' She'd been so hopeful that she'd find Beau. After all, how hard could it be in this day and age of the world wide web to find somebody? All she could find was his name in reference to the character in a movie—and that didn't do them any good.

'It's okay, hon.' Allegra put her arm around Maree's shoulders. 'I'll try a few more places.'

By the end of the day Allegra had trawled all the social media sites that she and Maree could think of. Allegra had sent a few messages to men with the same name that didn't have a photo included with their profile, hoping that one of them was him.

Over the next week there was a constant ache in her heart as she wondered what he was doing and whether he thought about her. She came to work every morning feeling a tremble of anticipation, hoping for good news from Allegra. But it didn't happen. Allegra would shake her head as yet another potential Beau Tennant replied.

·♥·♥·♥·♥·♥·

It was a Friday afternoon, a month since she met Beau and he'd turned her whole life upside down, when Allegra looked to Maree with a serious face. Maree had known it was coming, but still she'd been hoping to put off the talk for as long as possible. Maree kept staring at the computer, pretending she was working even though her eyes had gone out of focus five minutes ago.

'Don't you think it's a bit strange that we can't find any record of Beau anywhere? He's not even listed in his hometown phone directory.'

'Maybe he's really careful with his identity.' Maree shrugged irritably. 'With a movie coming out all.'

Allegra wasn't saying anything that she hadn't already thought in the silent hours of the night, when insomnia gripped her and she thought about him with an aching intensity. Where could he be? If Beau Tennant was his name there should be some way to track him down. They were living in the age of technology gone rife; it was easier than ever to find people you once knew. Allegra had tracked down her entire posse of high school girlfriends recently and they were planning a reunion. How could it be so hard to find one Beau Tennant?

You know why, the little voice in her head said.

'Still, there should be something,' Allegra said, stretching out the last word.

'He's a real person.'

'I'm not saying that he isn't. I'm just saying that he's not who he said he was.'

'Why would he lie?' Maree asked.

Allegra lifted her shoulder, her silent mime speaking for itself. Why did he lie about being a soldier? Why did he tell her he cared about her and then leave her behind like she was discarded trash?

Maree had been so sure of what they had. Their days together were like a kaleidoscope of color, full of shimmering possibilities. But now she was second-guessing herself. She had trusted everything he told her and now every word was turning out to be a lie.

'I need a coffee,' Maree muttered and escaped from the office, feeling near tears.

She stopped out on the street and found Beau's note in her bag, the paper creased from the countless times she'd re-read it. She'd tried so hard to convince herself that his confession was a gesture proving his noble intentions. But now she was beginning to believe that the only truth he had ever told her was in that first line, when he said he was a liar.

She didn't know what made a person like him want to hurt someone like her. Why he had deliberately and cold-heartedly made her care for him, only to destroy her, but there was no escaping the truth. She'd been duped. The man she thought she'd fallen in love with did not exist. Beau Tennant was nothing more than a figment of someone's imagination.

Hurt rushed through her veins, waking a hunger she'd thought was long gone. She'd only felt like this once before, when she had been arrested for DUI and her father didn't come. When she had realized that her father only cared for her as far as she affected his career, her body had cried out for the numbing power of alcohol. In the ten years since she had been brought low, she had had breakups, but she'd never felt this aching craving for the pain to stop.

Maree returned to the office, determined to focus on her work.

'Maree,' Allegra shrieked as she hung up the phone.

Her heart sped up with hope. It was Beau. Allegra had found him. He was real, and so was what they had.

'That was Richard Kincaid's assistant,' Allegra said.

Maree's heart sank again. What a fool she was to still hope despite all the evidence.

'Didn't you hear me?' Allegra shook her shoulders. 'He wants you to be his costume designer.'

'What?' Maree asked dazedly.

As she saw Allegra's smile, the fog lifted and she finally made sense of her words.

'He wants me?' Maree said slowly, as reality started sinking in.

'Yes.' Allegra grabbed her in a bear hug and started jumping. 'He wants you.'

She was saved. This part was her big break. She'd finally have the opportunity to use her creativity on a big budget movie.

More importantly, working on this movie would consume her and take away her hunger.

Chapter 9

'Are you sure about this?' Carter asked.

They were walking through the Alleno Studio lot to Tom's next meeting.

'I'm sure.'

He'd been counting down the days to his new job for the past two months and yet now that the day was finally here, all his certainty was gone. He wasn't sure if this was a good idea at all, but it wouldn't do to show his nerves to Carter. He'd been against this job and had tried to talk Tom out of it on numerous occasions.

'Because if this doesn't work it will all blow up in our faces,' Carter said.

He wasn't saying anything he hadn't repeated already, numerous times, so Tom just nodded. His hands were beginning to sweat and he felt butterflies in his stomach.

'We're here.' Carter stopped at the door.

Tom clenched his fists. This was the most important meeting of his life and yet he didn't know if he could walk through the door. He turned to Carter mutely.

Carter shook his head in exasperation. 'Break a leg,' he muttered under his breath as he opened the door and nudged Tom through and closed the door.

His heart beating fast, Tom turned around. He heard a noise and crouched. There was somebody under the table.

'Hello,' he called out.

There was a thud.

'Ouch,' a female voice muttered. She crawled out from under the table clutching her head.

'Are you all right?' Tom approached her side. The woman lifted her head and he felt shock like a punch to the solar plexus. He was looking at Maree's face. He hadn't recognized her from behind, the bountiful curves were gone. As he helped her stand up he was aware of how small she felt under his hand. She'd lost weight in the two months since they'd seen each other.

'I'm fine, thank you.' She pulled away. 'I'm Maree Reynard.'

'Tom Calvert.' He offered his hand. His muscles clenched as he waited to see if she would recognize him.

Carter had been telling him he was risking too much by letting Maree meet both Beau and Tom. If she realized they were one and the same and word leaked out he could ruin the premiere of *Heroes of Tennessee* when the announcement was supposed to be made. He'd told him to stay away from her, but Tom couldn't. He'd fallen for her, and the only thing that had sustained him during the past two months while he was filming as Beau was the knowledge that they would be working together on the movie *Ten Steps to the Moon*. He had originally turned the part down because he'd wanted a break after *Heroes of Tennessee*, but when he realized it was his chance to get Maree to go out with him as Tom, he'd had Carter negotiate that Maree become the costume designer.

'Oh, of course.' Maree shook his hand and introduced herself. 'I just need a moment and we can start your fitting.'

'Have we met before?' Tom said, not letting go when she tried to take her hand back. 'You look so familiar.'

Maree was clearly annoyed. She thought he was using a clichéd one-liner to come onto her.

'No, we've never met before,' Maree said firmly. 'Excuse me a sec.'

She lifted an eyebrow and, taking the hint, he let go of her hand.

Maree peered under the desk again. He bent with her and saw a pink paper in the far corner.

'I think we have,' Tom said. 'It was at the café on the Prime studio lot. I asked you to go to the Oliver Stone premiere with me.'

He was hoping that she would attribute any sense of recognition to this meeting, rather than to Beau.

Maree gave him a quick once over, an expression on her face as if she was looking at a pest.

'I'm sorry. I don't remember.' She smiled dismissively.

He felt deflated. This was going to be tougher than he thought.

Maree bent down to the floor and picked up the pink paper she'd been hunting for. As she came up she started to sway and Tom quickly reached out, grabbing hold of her waist to steady her. She became pale and her eyes fluttered closed as her legs gave out. He held her tightly, scooping his arm under her knees and lifting her up to hold her against his chest.

'Maree, Maree,' he called her name, but she was dead weight in his arms.

He carried her to the couch in the corner and laid her down. He found a cloth and ran some water over it. Returning to her side, he dabbed the damp cloth against her forehead. He noticed how pale her skin looked, and the dark circles under her eyes. What had she been doing to herself?

Nothing that you didn't do either, Tom thought. For the two months they had been apart he'd felt like he had a constant ache in his chest. Guilt and infatuation warred inside him until he felt a broken man. Ken Grey, his director for *Heroes of Tennessee,* had loved seeing the devastation wreaked on his body. He'd been full of compliments about Tom's method acting and his ability to immerse himself into Beau's persona.

At any other time in his life Tom would have enjoyed receiving such praise from a director of Ken's caliber, but all he'd felt was impatience for the shoot to be over so he could finally see Maree and try to win her back. And now here they were, and yet everything was different to what he'd hoped.

She started to stir and her eyes opened.

'Thank God you're awake,' Tom said. 'How are you feeling? Should I call a doctor?'

'No, no, I'm fine,' Maree said, waving him away. She tried to sit up, but she didn't have the energy.

Tom put his arm under her and lifted her to sit.

'I just forgot to eat,' Maree said.

'Are you sure?' Tom asked. 'You're not pregnant, are you?'

The thought filled him with horror. He didn't know what he would do if she was pregnant with Beau's child. How would he ever be able to make something like that right?

Maree laughed. 'Why would you think that?'

'I don't know,' Tom shrugged. 'It seems like it's usually pregnant women who faint.'

Relief settled on him. At least that was one thing he didn't have to worry about.

'I just haven't been eating or sleeping much lately.'

'So that's why you look like a walking scarecrow,' Tom said dryly.

'Jeez, thanks. Always appreciate honesty from a stranger.'

Tom smoothed her hair away from her face. 'That's not what I meant. I mean you don't look well.'

'And how would you know?' Maree pushed his hand away.

Without realizing it, he'd slipped into an easy familiarity with her, but to her he was a stranger.

Maree turned green. 'Ow.' She clutched her stomach.

'What's wrong?' Tom asked. 'Are you sure you're not pregnant?'

'I'm not pregnant,' she snapped. 'If you must know I just had my period. I'm just hungry.'

'Why didn't you say so!' He handed her the cloth. 'Here, hold this against your face. I'll get you some food.'

Tom left the room. He needed some time to re-think his strategy. When he had dreamed about this moment he'd always imagined there would be a connection between them, an echo of the feelings that she had for Beau, and that establishing a relationship again would be effortless. Instead she was prickly and standoffish toward Tom.

He hadn't realized how deep Maree's defenses were toward actors. He reached the café and ordered. He had three months to prove himself to her, to get her to like him for a start, and maybe, if he was lucky, to win her heart. But he knew that once he told her the real truth about Beau, that was going to be a hell of a lot harder.

·❤·❤·❤·❤·❤·

'There's no—' Maree didn't get the chance to finish her sentence and tell Tom there was no need for him to get food. The door banged as he left the room.

She tried to get up when he left. She had to start on the fitting as soon as he returned, but her body felt so heavy and uncoordinated. She walked over to the sketchbook and opened it so she could show him her designs, but it felt like her hand didn't belong to her. Each movement felt as though she was doing it underwater.

She noticed the invitation next to her sketchbook. Allegra's party. She groaned. Perhaps if she hadn't met up with Allegra this morning, none of this would have happened.

Maree had waved at Allegra who was waiting for her in front of the café. They were having a coffee to catch up. In the two months since Maree had resigned from *The Time of Our*

Lives they'd emailed sporadically and tried to meet weekly, but this was their first face-to-face in three weeks. When Maree reached Allegra, they hugged. They'd worked together for six years and Maree had felt like a limb was missing since she left her old job.

'You have to eat more and get some sleep,' Allegra scolded, as she pulled away and looked at her. 'You're wasting away.'

'Yes, Mom.' Maree forced a wan smile as she sat listlessly on the stool in front of her.

Allegra had already ordered for them. Maree lifted her cup of coffee. Her hand trembled and she quickly put the coffee down and placed her hand on her lap, thankful Allegra was getting extra sugar sachets at the counter. Maybe she did need to eat more. She tried to cast her mind back to the last time she'd had a proper meal. All she could remember was snacking while standing in the production office kitchenette. Food was pretty scarce at home too and she'd buy meals on the run, eating half and tossing the rest.

'So what's on the agenda today?' Allegra asked when she returned, eager for details of how her new job was coming along.

'Today I start the wardrobe fittings with the stars,' Maree said.

'Yay, can't wait to hear the gossip. Make sure you remember everything and clue me in on Friday.'

'Friday?' Maree asked.

'My birthday.' Allegra slapped her hand. 'Don't you dare forget.'

Maree hadn't been very interested in the outside world. She'd blown off Allegra's numerous invitations and in her last email Allegra had put her foot down. It was time for Maree to re-join the rest of the world and start acting like a friend, or else. Maree wasn't willing to test the 'or else' option.

'I won't.' Maree smiled brightly, while inside she panicked. What did she do with the invitation? She remembered taking it from Allegra. Usually she would hang it on the fridge and carefully pencil the date in her diary, but in the past couple of months her life had taken on a certain chaotic quality.

'How are you doing with other stuff?' Allegra squeezed her hand.

Other stuff was code for Beau. He had ripped a hole in her life and the only thing that had kept her going was the movie she was going to be working on. Her heartbreak had made her more productive, and she used her insomnia-filled nights to design and create outfits.

'I'm okay.' Maree took another sip of coffee, the caffeine giving her a much needed jolt of energy. 'Keeping busy helps.'

As she prepared for pre-production, Beau had drifted from her thoughts slightly. She still felt pain and still thought about him, but she had been able to forget about him for lengths of time as she immersed herself in the director's vision for the movie.

'Well, maybe you'll find someone else to occupy your time at my birthday.' Allegra smiled wickedly. 'I'm going to have lots of eye-candy there for you to choose from.'

Maree groaned internally. She should have known that Allegra had a secondary motive. Her idea of dating was like a giant daisy chain where she got over one man by latching onto another.

'I don't know if I'm ready for that.'

Allegra's face turned serious. 'The bastard took something away from you. He took away your confidence and you need to get it back.' She refused to use Beau's name. Instead she always referred to him as 'the bastard.' 'I'm not asking you to date. I just want you to have fun again.'

Allegra was always so melodramatic that sometimes Maree forgot how perceptive she was. She was right, Beau had shaken her confidence. Finding out that she had been duped so thoroughly had made her doubt herself in a way she never had before. Ever since she'd been running scared, and had done everything she could to fill up her time so she didn't have to think. The movie hadn't even started and she was already feeling burned out. Maybe Allegra was right and it was time to get some balance back in her life.

'I could use some fun,' Maree said.

Allegra laughed. 'Now that's what I'm talking about.' She reached over and squeezed her arm. 'We are going to have a epic night for my twenty-fifth birthday.'

Maree lifted an eyebrow. 'Twenty-fifth?' Allegra was a year older than her and Maree was twenty-eight.

'It's my party and I've decided I'm going to sit on twenty-five for a while.'

Maree shook her head as she laughed. Trust Allegra to try and stop the laws of nature.

'All right then.' Maree lifted her coffee and they clinked cups. 'To your twenty-fifth birthday.'

'Woo hoo,' Allegra cheered.

Maree felt her spirits lift a little. She was looking forward to tomorrow night.

When she'd returned to her office she began rifling through her papers, looking for the invite, when there was a knock on the door.

'I'll just be a sec,' she'd said, spying a corner of pink paper between the table and wall. As she tried to get it out, it fell under the desk. 'Dammit,' she cursed as she crawled under the table.

She heard someone call out her name and bumped her head on the table as she jerked up. When she crawled out she saw the handsome actor who was playing the lead had arrived for his meeting. After they exchanged introductions he tried the old 'Have we met before' line.

Maree fought to keep from rolling her eyes. He was going to be one of those. The Letch was what she and Allegra had dubbed the actors who thought they were God's gift and used their clichéd one-liners to score.

Maree noticed Allegra's invitation and bent to the floor to pick it up. Thank God. Now she wouldn't have to call Allegra and confess her carelessness.

Tom Calvert was talking, but Maree didn't hear what he was saying. Her head swam and blackness started filling her vision. She felt herself sinking to the floor and suddenly strong arms were around her.

Concerned blue eyes looked into hers. 'Maree, Maree,' Tom called her name.

He did look familiar, Maree thought.

When she awoke she was lying on the couch. She blinked open her eyes and saw him bent over her with a worried frown. She felt something cool, and realized he was pressing a damp cloth to her face.

Maree came back to the present when her office door opened and Tom walked in again, carrying a paper bag and two cups. 'Why are you standing?' he asked. He put the bag and cups on the table and led her back to the couch, sitting her down. 'What would have happened if you fainted again? You could have fallen and hurt your head,' he scolded.

Maree was bemused by his fussing, but too tired to question anything.

He held out a sandwich. 'Eat.' He watched her as she took a bite.

'Would you mind not doing that?' she asked, after she'd finished chewing.

'What?'

'Staring at me while I eat.'

'Oh, sure.' He reached for a coffee cup and took off the lid. After stirring in two sugars he handed it to her.

'How did you know I take two sugars?' Maree asked.

'I don't. I just thought you'd need the sugar to give you a boost.' He waited for her to have a few sips before taking it back. 'Now keep eating,' he commanded.

After she lifted an eyebrow he sighed and looked away again. He caught sight of the sketchbook. 'Is this Rex's outfit?' Rex was his character in *Ten Steps to the Moon*.

Maree nodded. 'I was trying—'

'Talk after you eat,' Tom said briskly.

Chastened, Maree finished her sandwich while he flipped through her designs.

'I like them. I'm just not sure about this one.' He turned back a few pages to a space-age outfit.

'That's for the judgment scene,' Maree said. 'He's put in that uniform when he's presented to the judges in the altar room.'

'Yes, but it looks a bit too *Tour de France* for me.' He noticed she'd finished her sandwich and handed her a bag of candy.

'No, thanks. I'm full,' Maree said.

'I don't care. You need sugar to give you an energy boost.'

Maree wanted to tell him to jump, but there was something so implacable in the cast of his gaze that she meekly accepted the jelly beans offered and ate a few.

'Thanks. I'm feeling much better. I guess we'd better get started.' She went to push herself off the couch when the door opened.

'I'm here for the fitting,' said the tall blonde who stepped in. 'Hello.' She smiled widely when she saw Tom. Emma Corn was playing Susan, Rex's love interest in the movie. 'It's good to see you again.'

'You too.' Tom nodded briskly before turning back to Maree. 'We'll have to pick this up another time. You text me when you want to meet.' He picked up her phone and bumped them together, so their numbers transferred to each other's phone.

'I'm so excited about filming.' Emma grabbed his arm as he passed.

'Me too.' Tom gently patted her hand before removing it. 'Until next time, Maree,' he said, before walking out of the office.

Emma gave her a questioning look, confused at being fobbed off so swiftly. Obviously this did not happen often to someone who looked like her.

'Shall we get started?' Maree picked up her measuring tape.

She spent the rest of the day with a smile on her face whenever she remembered Tom's quiet competence and compassion as he took care of her. Usually she was careful to keep the actors she worked with at a distance, but something about the way he had been so calm and reassuring made her feel comfortable around him.

Be careful, Maree. Don't let one moment of vulnerability cloud your judgment. She wiped the smile off her face. She had to keep focused on her career. Tom was still a stranger, and he had to stay that way.

When she got home that night she felt her stomach stirring with hunger for the first time in weeks. She opened her fridge and was greeted with one limp stick of celery, green cheese, and something that once was yogurt. 'Oh God,' she held her nose as she threw them in the trash and then took the bag outside.

As she was washing her hands she heard her phone beeping. She opened the text message. 'Eat Dinner!!!' It was from Tom.

Maree didn't know whether to feel happy or annoyed at his high-handedness. She spent a few seconds deliberating over her reply. How could she politely acknowledge him, without encouraging him further?

'Will do,' she finally replied and left the apartment for the shopping strip. She'd eat some Chinese and then go grocery shopping. It was time she took Allegra's advice and joined the land of the living. The first order of business was to take care of herself better. Tomorrow night it was about getting some fun back in her life.

Chapter 10

Tom eyed the stairs leading to the private function area of the club as he sipped his glass of water. He had to keep his head clear if he was going to implement his plan. Emma twirled in front of him, smiling widely as she danced.

Tom nodded politely.

'You're not dancing,' she leaned forward and spoke in his ear. She had to shout to be heard above the dance music booming through the speakers.

'I'm not much of a dancer,' Tom shouted back. That wasn't the truth. He loved dancing, but he had to make sure he didn't miss Maree.

Emma started moving her hips. She was wearing a mini-dress with spaghetti straps, her bountiful cleavage bouncing as she moved.

'Excuse me,' Tom said, and walked toward the bathroom.

He'd known it was a risk to arrange a party for all of the cast. He'd touted it as a 'meet and greet', but his real goal was to use it as a cover so he could be at the club Maree was going to.

He'd seen the invitation to her friend's birthday party and taken it as an opportunity to try and spend time with Maree in a social setting. But in the half hour since they'd arrived Emma had been blatantly flirting with him and he was running out of excuses to deflect her.

He climbed the stairs to the second level and leaned against a pillar so he was hidden from view. He watched Maree talking to a woman dressed like a 1950s diva who Tom assumed was Allegra. Maree was smiling widely and looking like the woman he'd fallen for. The tension she'd carried when he saw her for the fitting was fading away, as if she was taking off a too-tight coat.

He felt as nervous as if he was spying on his first crush. His whole plan was to casually bump into Maree and hope that the spark they had felt for each other could be reignited. He hadn't thought any further than that, but now as he watched her in her red silk dress, the bodice tight and the skirt floating around her legs, his stomach clenched with desire. All he could think about was their night together, and he wanted more.

Get your act together, Calvert. You're in this for the long game.

Maree and her friends stood and went downstairs to the dance floor. He noticed Emma still dancing in the crowd, her head swiveling as she searched for him. Damn. He was going to have to deal with her tonight.

He went downstairs again and merged with the crowd on the dance floor. As he danced he was aware of where Maree was, as if they were on the same radio frequency. He maneuvered his way closer to her and knew the moment that she recognized him, but he acted cool, keeping his attention on his dance partner, a petite redhead who had killer moves. The redhead eventually moved off and merged back into the crowd and Tom lifted his head. He saw Maree straight ahead and smiled as if it was the first time he was seeing her.

Her dance partner was wearing black leather pants and a white silk shirt. He was gyrating and trying to draw her into a two-step, but Maree was blocking him with her arm movements.

Tom danced toward her. 'Hi,' he shouted in her ear, forcing Leather Pants to step away.

Maree looked relieved at Leather Pants' retreat. 'Hello.'

'Do you come here often?' he asked, smelling the vanilla scent of her hair as he spoke in her ear.

She shook her head and pointed to Allegra. 'I'm here for a birthday party.' She had to step close to him as he turned his ear toward her, her chest almost pressing against his as she pushed herself up to reach. 'You?'

'My cast mates organized a meet and greet party,' Tom said. Maree nodded.

As they danced Tom made sure that he kept a distance between them so she didn't think he was making a move. He saw her relax and let go. Now that he was with Maree he was finally able to be in the moment and enjoy the music. He loved dancing and the feeling of being invisible on a crowded dance floor.

They danced to a few songs, their bodies naturally finding their own rhythm. Eventually Maree mimed that she was thirsty. Tom nodded and followed her off the dance floor. He asked her what she wanted to drink and pushed his way to the bar. When he got their drinks they found a table and sat on the stools.

'You're looking better,' he said. There was a flush of color on her cheeks.

'I'm feeling great.' She finished her margarita in a few gulps.

'I hope you ate tonight,' Tom said.

Maree laughed. 'I did. Thank you.' She reached out and rubbed his shoulder. 'You're being very kind to me.'

Tom realized she was drunk. Maree wouldn't be so touchy-feely otherwise. 'I'm a kind person.'

Maree laughed again. 'Are you going to drink that?' She nodded toward his untouched whiskey and soda.

He shook his head. She picked up the glass and started to drink.

'Maybe you should slow down,' he suggested.

'I don't think so. Tonight's my first night out for months and I'm going to have fun until I hurt.'

'You keep drinking like that and you'll hurt a lot tomorrow,' Tom said.

'Good.' A shadow crossed her face. 'I'd like to feel pain some-where else.' She touched her chest.

'Ah, the pain of a breakup?' he asked. His body tensed as he waited to hear what she would say about Beau.

'It was more like a hit and run.'

Tom's stomach dropped at the bitterness in her voice. What had he done? He knew that he'd hurt her by leaving, but being confronted with the magnitude of her pain was agonizing.

'I'm sure he's hurting too,' Tom said.

'I'm sure he's not.' Maree finished off the whiskey. She smiled again. 'So who were you hoping to meet and greet tonight?'

His heart tightened in his chest at the way she was putting on a cheerful front. All he could do was play along. 'I'm here strictly in a professional capacity.' Tom placed his hand over his heart.

'Really? Does she know that?' Maree nodded toward the dance floor.

Emma was in their line of vision and was watching them closely. She was using her dance partner as a pole as she gyrated down to the floor and back up again. Seeing that she'd caught Tom's eye, Emma left her dance partner and walked toward him.

Tom looked at Maree for help.

'I think I'll enjoy the show.' Maree laughed and shooed him onto the dance floor.

Emma reached him and yanked his arm, almost dragging him up. Maree waved at him and continued sipping his whiskey. He had his hands full trying to keep his distance from Emma as they danced.

Maree came onto the dance floor and kept her eyes on Tom's. She was dancing loosely, her whole body moving in a sensual rhythm. She nudged Emma out of the way and placed her hands on his chest as she shouted in his ear. 'I'm here to save you.'

Emma flounced off and danced with another partner next to them.

There was a look in Maree's eyes and Tom knew that she'd crossed over the line from tipsy to drunk. She stroked his chest.

He took her hands and gently removed them, under the pretext of dancing.

She leaned her forward and her lips brushed against his. He wanted nothing more than to sink into her, but he couldn't. He'd already taken advantage of her as Beau, he wasn't going to do it as Tom.

'You don't want to do this.'

'Why not?' she demanded.

'You've had too much to drink.'

'I know,' Maree drawled. 'That's why I'm doing this.' She kissed his jaw.

He gripped his hands around her shoulders and moved her away. 'No.'

She blinked her eyes. 'Okay.'

'No, that's not what I meant. I think you're beautiful.' He smoothed her hair away from her face. 'But I can't take advantage of you like this.'

Maree held herself stiffly and nodded. 'Thank you for your concern.' She walked off the dance floor and toward the bathroom.

He started to follow, but Emma grabbed hold of his arm and yanked him back. 'Now you're all mine, lover boy.'

'Listen, I think you're great, but I'm taking a break from dating.'

Emma looked at him with confusion.

'It's not you, it's me.'

'I know it is,' Emma said.

'You see, I'm in love with someone else. I'm sorry, I have to go.'

Tom left her to go look for Maree. He walked to the back of the club, passing by the soft couches that were strategically placed in pockets of darkness, allowing patrons privacy for their nefarious activities. He spotted Leather Pants and Maree sitting together against the back wall. Leather Pants leaned forward and started mashing his lips against Maree.

Tom felt a burst of rage. He wanted to punch Leather Pants in the face for daring to touch his woman, but he had to control the urge. His priority was to take care of Maree, and if he was arrested he wouldn't be able to do that.

He reached them and called her name.

Leather Pants looked up. 'Do you mind?'

'Yes, I do.' Tom bit out the words, his hands fisted by his side.

As Maree looked up at him her face cleared, like she was waking from a dream. 'Oh, God.' She covered her mouth, horror filling her eyes.

'Let's go.' Tom held out his hand.

Her hand was shaking as she reached out and clasped his. He helped her up and as they walked through the dance floor and toward the door, Allegra spotted them.

'What happened?' she demanded as she peered into Maree's face.

'She's had too much to drink,' said Tom. 'I'll take her home.'

Allegra looked torn.

'It's okay.' Maree forced a smile for her friend's benefit. 'I just need to sleep it off. Happy birthday.' She gave Allegra a hug and then stepped back beside Tom.

He automatically curled his arm around her waist and walked out with her. He'd hoped that they would leave together at the end of the night, but not like this. He looked down at the top of Maree's head and felt crushing guilt. He knew she would be hurt by Beau's defection, but he didn't realize the extent of her devastation.

As they stepped out of the club flashbulbs assaulted them. 'Who's your girlfriend, Tom?'

Tom stiffened as he recognized the voice. Norman Keller was a paparazzo who had dogged his every move since he'd made it into the big time. Norman had been at the club when Tom was caught with cocaine and was the reason that the story broke.

'Who's that?' Maree muttered.

'Just the paparazzi,' Tom said.

'How long have you been dating Tom?' Norman asked Maree as he fell into step beside them, shooting close-ups of her.

Tom hunched her deeper under his arm, trying to cover her face. He knew she hated the paparazzi as much as he did and she didn't say anything more. She just tried to keep up with Tom's brisk pace, but she was struggling. Tom held her tighter around the waist, supporting her so she could match his pace.

'Are you going to his house for a nightcap?' Norman threw himself in front of them, shooting their faces as they walked toward him.

Tom didn't falter, just lifted his arm up so his elbow was facing outward. Norman jumped out of the way just as Tom's elbow was about to hit his face.

Tom helped Maree into the car, trying to shield her from the flashbulbs. She was looking pale and beads of sweat had formed on her face.

Norman was still calling out questions, each one more obnoxious than the last. He was trying to get a reaction. Tom went to the driver's side and got in, ignoring Norman who was shadowing him. Early on he'd made the mistake of reacting with anger and given the tabloids a feeding frenzy; now he'd learned that silence was his best defense.

Tom carefully pulled out onto the street. He noticed Norman's car dropping in behind them. 'Dammit,' he muttered under his breath. If he drove Maree home, Norman would have her address and would stalk her in an effort to get information about him.

'Maree, we have to go to my house,' Tom said.

She didn't respond. He glanced over and saw she was looking distressed.

'I think I'm going to be sick,' she said.

'Can you hold on for ten minutes?' If he hit the pedal hard he'd be home quicker.

She covered her mouth with her hand, her eyes becoming wide as she hunched over.

Tom quickly pulled over to the side of the road. Maree jumped out of the car and before he'd cut the engine she was bent over and vomiting. Headlights lit up the car cabin. Tom threw open the door and almost ran to the car behind him. He reached the driver's door just as it was opening, and pushed it shut. 'Wind down your window.'

Norman already had the camera in his hand, pointing it toward Tom. Tom felt sick as he saw the enjoyment in Norman's eyes. He was hoping Tom would assault him and he could capture the footage.

'Listen,' Tom said, moderating his voice, 'my date is sick and I don't want you to take photos of her in this condition.'

'I thought you had the magic touch with women, and now I find out your company makes them sick.' Norman laughed at his own wit.

Tom's fists clenched. He made sure to keep them out of sight under the window.

'I was hoping we could make a deal.' Tom continued as if Norman hadn't spoken.

'I thought you didn't make deals with the likes of me,' Norman said.

Some celebrities were known for courting the attention of the paparazzi. They staged run-ins to coincide with a movie premiere, but Tom had never played that game.

'Well, now I am. Do you want in or not?' Tom asked.

Norman's expression became calculating. 'So is this one a keeper?' He nodded toward Maree who was lit up by his headlights. She was standing and holding herself up on the passenger door.

Tom had never before shown any concern about his dates being photographed. He'd just assumed that they would consider a tabloid photograph of them together as a souvenir, but he knew Maree wasn't like that. She would be horrified that she'd come to the attention of the paparazzi. While he couldn't do anything about all the photographers outside of the club, he could make sure that she wasn't humiliated by a picture of her being sick on the side of the road.

Tom turned back toward Norman. 'Leave now and you'll be able to find me surfing tomorrow at Malibu.'

The paparazzi were always looking for an exclusive, and Tom knew that a beach shot would give Norman a pay day.

Norman smiled and put down his camera. 'You've got a deal.'

Tom stepped away and watched until Norman's car merged onto the freeway. Maree was already in the car by the time he'd walked back.

'Are you okay?' he asked after he'd slid into the driver's seat.

Maree nodded and leaned her head against the headrest with her eyes closed. When they reached his house, Tom helped her out of the car, and scooped her arm around his neck as he almost carried her into the house.

'You can stay here tonight,' he said when they reached the guest bedroom and he had sat her down on the bed.

'I need a shower,' she said.

Tom went into the bathroom and got the water running. When he returned, Maree was standing, twisting in a circle as she tried to reach the zip on her back.

'I'll help.' He turned her around and undid the zip. 'I'll just be outside.'

'Okay.' She threw off the dress and went to take a step, but lost her balance.

Tom caught her before she fell. 'I think I'm going to have to help you have a shower.' In her condition she could fall and get a concussion.

'Okay.' She looked up at him with the innocent eyes of a child.

He realized that she was too blasted to know what was going on. 'Let's go.'

She followed him docilely into the bathroom, and he guided her into the shower. She was still wearing her red bra and bikini panties. He helped her wash her hair, then handed her the soap to wash herself. After she rinsed off he turned off the water and helped her out, wrapping her in a towel. Her eyes were closed and she smiled softly as he towel-dried her hair.

'I'll get you a T-shirt to sleep in,' he said when he'd led her back to the bedroom.

When he returned with a T-shirt she was lying on the bed on top of the covers.

'Maree, Maree,' he urged as he sat her up. 'Put your hands up.' He pulled the T-shirt down over her head and unhooked her bra behind her back. Even though they had made love, it felt wrong to look at her when she was so vulnerable. He took her bra off through the T-shirt sleeve and helped her under the covers.

'I need you to take off your panties,' Tom said.

Maree frowned. He saw her shimmying under the covers as she took them off and handed them to him. She turned on her side and with a deep sigh, she fell asleep. The desire he always felt when he was around her was muted by tenderness. All he wanted to do was lie down with her and just hold her, but he couldn't. The next time they made love was going to be when she knew everything. He wasn't going to take advantage of her again.

He picked up her dress off the floor and turned off the light before leaving the room.

Chapter 11

When Maree woke in an unfamiliar bed and with a throbbing hangover, she broke out into a cold sweat. Oh, God. She'd done it again. She'd had a one night stand. When she looked under the covers it only confirmed her fears. She was wearing a T-shirt and nothing else.

She peered around the room, but she was alone. Who had she gone home with? She couldn't remember. She clutched her head as she tried to force the memories. She remembered arriving at the club and meeting Allegra. She'd ordered a margarita and drunk it all.

The warmth of the alcohol had spread through her, loosening her muscles and making her feel relaxed and happy. She'd been so lonely since Beau walked out of her life; the pain of losing him had numbed her to all other emotions. This was the first time that she'd felt something resembling joy. She'd had a few more drinks and ended up on the dance floor with the guy Allegra had set her up with for the night. A leather-pants-wearing stuntman whose name she couldn't remember, but who looked like he could moonlight with the Chippendale strippers.

She had an image of Tom Calvert flirting with her. She remembered kissing a man. His face wasn't clear and as they were kissing she'd felt outside of her body and she wasn't sure if it was what she wanted. But he was a good kisser, and she'd enjoyed the feeling of being held and being wanted. Beau rejecting her had made her feel so unloved and she was tired of feeling an empty void.

Maree's eyes snapped open. She'd been kissing the stuntman! She remembered his ponytail brushing against her skin and tickling her as they kissed and now she was going to have to face him in the cold light of day—ugh! She sat up in bed and looked around for her clothes. Her plan was to get dressed and sneak out without having to deal with the awkward morning-after conversation.

But her clothes were nowhere to be found. All she could find was a white flannel dressing gown hanging off the back of the bathroom door. After she did some damage control by repairing her hair and making herself vaguely presentable, she returned to the bedroom.

She couldn't believe that she was in this situation again—doing the walk of shame at her age. She took a deep breath and opened the bedroom door, then headed toward the sound of clanging pots. She was just going to have to bluster her way out of this somehow. As soon as she got her clothes she was calling a taxi and getting the hell out of here. The only thing making the situation bearable was that she was still feeling the dulling effects of alcohol.

When she entered the kitchen she smelled eggs cooking. A man was standing behind the open door of the fridge and only his jean-clad legs were visible. The door closed to reveal Tom Calvert, his blue eyes staring right at her.

'You,' she said. She'd worked herself up to greeting the stuntman. How the hell had she ended up going home with Tom Calvert?

'You're awake.' He smiled and gestured toward the kitchen bench. 'I was just going to bring you breakfast in bed.' There was a tray with scrambled eggs, toast, and orange juice.

'Thank you.' Maree didn't know what to think.

'Here, take a seat.'

She was glad to sit down, her legs feeling suddenly unsteady. Tom brought her a cup of coffee and she sipped slowly as she tried to remember last night.

'How are you feeling?' He sat across from her, leaning on his elbows as he sipped his coffee.

'My head is throbbing, but otherwise I'm okay.'

'Oh, good. I thought after all the action by the side of the road that you'd be sore today.'

Oh my God. What had she done? Had they had sex outdoors?

'Side of the road?' Maree repeated, her voice high-pitched.

'I was hoping you could hold out until we got to my house, but you were desperate.'

Maree gasped. 'I certainly was not. Just because I hadn't had sex in two months, didn't mean I was desperate.' She stood up. 'And I find it hard to believe that I wanted to have sex by the side of the road.'

Tom leaned back, his brow furrowing in confusion. 'We didn't have sex.'

'But you just said—'

'I said you couldn't wait to get to the house—because you had to throw up.'

'What?' Maree felt waves of humiliation wash over her.

His shoulders started to shake, but it wasn't until she heard a snort that she realized he was laughing.

'It's not funny,' she snapped.

His eyes twinkled as he bit his lip. 'You're right. It's not funny.' He was holding himself rigidly, trying not to laugh.

As she replayed their conversation she covered her face with her hands and now her shoulders started to shake.

'It's okay.' Tom patted her on the arm. 'I'm sorry I laughed.'

He sounded so contrite, that she started to shake harder. She uncovered her face and looked at him.

'Action by the side of the road,' she gasped between spurts of laughter.

He started laughing again too. 'Well, I didn't want to say because of your projectile vomiting.'

Maree started laughing harder. While it was anything but funny that she found herself in Tom Calvert's kitchen and couldn't remember how she got there, the farcical nature of the whole thing meant she couldn't do anything but laugh.

Their splutters died down and Maree had to wipe her eyes. As she sat back on the stool, her stomach muscles hurt from laughing, and probably from vomiting the night before.

'How did I get here?' she asked.

'What's the last thing you remember?'

'You and I were having a drink together, I think. Then Emma dragged you onto the dance floor and everything is blurry after that.'

'You had a few more drinks after that.' Tom pushed the tray of food toward her. 'I was giving you a lift home, but you got sick and then passed out in the car so I brought you here.'

'Thank you.' Maree took a mouthful of the eggs. They were beautifully light and fluffy. As she ate she had a flash of an image of her and Tom almost kissing. 'So you were taking me to my place so ...'

She found it hard to believe that he'd been so full of noble intentions and was taking her home out of the goodness of his heart.

'So you could sleep.'

'Then why did I wake up wearing only a T-shirt?' Maree demanded.

'You had a shower before you went to bed.' Tom was wiping the bench as he answered.

'By myself?'

Tom didn't say anything. The sponge in his hand suddenly held his interest.

'Did you help me shower?' Dread was climbing through her again. She couldn't believe that he'd seen her naked and she couldn't even remember. How much did she drink last night?

It's not the quantity, it's the fact that you haven't drunk anything more than a glass of wine in ten years.

'Don't worry, I was able to control myself.' His voice held an edge.

She opened her mouth to ask more, and quickly closed it. Maybe it was better that she didn't ask any more questions.

'I would never take advantage of you, Maree.'

Maree arched an eyebrow. 'Because I was drunk?'

'No. Because I'm looking for more than a one night stand.'

Maree smiled.

'You don't believe me?'

She remained silent.

'You sound very suspicious of the opposite sex. Just because you got hurt—'

'How do you know that?' Maree demanded.

'You told me.'

That must have been when they were talking at the club. She made a mental note never to get drunk again.

'I know it's hard getting over a bad breakup—'

'Really?' Maree asked. 'And you know so much about bad breakups because you've inflicted so many of them?'

'I've had my share of heartbreak,' Tom said.

'I find that very hard to believe,' Maree said wryly.

'Why? Because I look like this you think I can't feel emotion?' Tom snapped.

Maree was surprised, but quickly rallied. He sounded almost bitter about his looks. 'People who look like you usually get a free pass. You get who you want, when you want, without exerting any effort at all.'

He broke eye contact. A movie star like him had his pick of beautiful women, all eager to play the game of casual sex partner in exchange for a photo opportunity in a tabloid magazine and the profile boost that came with it. And he'd probably enjoyed his time with the women while it lasted and not wasted a second thought on them once he'd moved on.

'That's what I thought.' Maree sipped her orange juice.

'Even though I've been careless it doesn't mean I haven't been in love and lost that love. I know the pain of wanting someone so much that every fiber of your being hurts, but not being able to have them because of your own stupid arrogance.'

He quickly looked away and blinked. He sounded so heartbroken, and her heart softened. *He's an actor, Maree. Don't be stupid.*

'Thanks for the eggs.' Maree took her plate to the sink and started to rinse it.

'It's okay.' Tom took the plate off her. 'I'll do that.' He squirted dishwashing liquid onto the sponge and started washing the plate. 'Your dress is in the laundry room.' Tom pointed to the door next to them.

Maree opened the door and took the coathanger hanging on a hook. 'Can I use your phone to call a taxi?'

'I'll give you a lift.'

'That's okay. I've put you out enough.'

'I insist,' Tom said. 'After all, I promised I'd take you home and I have yet to keep that promise.'

Maree sighed and nodded. She just wanted to get home, at this point she didn't care how she got there.

As she dressed in the guest bedroom she tried to piece together what had happened after they left the club. She remembered feeling dizzy and ill in the car. And there was a vague image of her stepping out of a shower and feeling cozy and snug as someone wrapped a towel around her and dried her.

Was that Tom? Could he have really been such a gentleman? She was so confused. Why had he been so kind to her? Although perhaps he'd just been stuck. They'd probably left the club together, but she'd gotten sick on the drive home, putting a stop to their plans. That still didn't explain why he didn't drop her off at her home and leave her to her own devices. Instead he'd brought her to his house and taken care of her.

She went to the bathroom and checked herself in the mirror. The dress was freshly ironed without a crease in it. She was confused. He had brought her home, helped her shower, washed her clothes and ironed her dress. Who did that? A suspicion formed, but she quickly dismissed it.

Just because a man washes clothes and irons them doesn't mean he's gay.

Tom was waiting for her by the front door when she returned. He opened the door and she passed by him. There was a white envelope on the ground. Maree picked it up and handed it to him. 'This must be for you.'

Tom opened it. His body stiffened.

'What's wrong?' Maree asked.

'It's another message from my stalker,' he sighed.

She was reminded again why she didn't want to date actors. There was always some behind-the-scenes drama.

Tom looked warily around the street as he walked her to the car. Maree gave him directions as they drove, and twenty minutes later he pulled up in her driveway. She still felt shaky and weak from her hangover. She couldn't wait to get inside and lie on the couch for the rest of the day.

'Thanks for everything.' She reached for the door handle.

'I'll walk you to your door.' Tom turned off the engine and got out. He came around to the passenger side and offered her his arm, walking her to the door. 'I'll see you Monday,' he said.

Maree blanked out. Did she agree to go out on another date with him?

'I don't think we should see each other again—' she started, wanting to let him down easy.

'We have an appointment for my fitting.'

Maree flushed. Could this day get any more embarrassing? 'Of course.'

Tom started to lean toward her. Oh, God. He was going to kiss her. Of course he wasn't gay. She turned her head. His lips brushed against hers and he jerked back like he'd been electrocuted. He'd been aiming for her cheek.

'Sorry,' he said.

'No, I'm sorry.' She flushed again. What was wrong with her?

Tom offered his hand. 'Monday.'

'Yes.' Maree shook his hand, staring at his chest. She couldn't meet his eyes.

She only looked up when he turned away, and watched him walk to his car, admiring the curve of his butt. He really was handsome. It was such a shame if he was gay.

He turned, catching her leering at him. She flushed again and quickly stepped into the house, nearly tripping over her feet in the process. How was she ever going to look him in the face again?

·❤·❤·❤·❤·❤·

Maree spent the rest of the weekend lying on the couch, watching movies and eating toast with tea as her stomach recovered. On Monday morning she was at work early. Emma arrived for her fitting, bubbling with good cheer and talking a mile a minute.

Maree was painfully aware of the ticking of the clock. Her next appointment was with Tom and she didn't know how she was going to face him after the weekend. She kept remembering he'd seen her vomiting and seen her naked. She didn't know which was more humiliating.

Emma was scrolling through her phone while Maree was fitting her. 'Hey, you're famous.' She tilted the phone toward Maree.

On screen was a photo of Maree sitting in Tom's car as he pulled out of the car park at the club. She noticed the hyperlink belonging to a trashy tabloid.

'Unbelievable,' Maree muttered. 'Nothing happened.'

'Of course not.' Emma shrugged as she looked at herself in the full-length mirror. She was wearing a space-age tunic Maree had designed, the shimmery material molding to her curves and leaving nothing to the imagination.

'What do you mean?' Maree asked.

'Don't you remember Friday night?'

Maree looked at her blankly.

'I made a move on him after you, and he did the 'it's not you, it's me' speech.'

Maree had a quick flash of trying to kiss Tom, but he'd turned away. Was it true? Had she come onto him on Friday night?

'Apparently, he's in love with 'someone." Emma made quotation marks with her fingers. 'And you know what that means.' She sighed. 'Whoever he is, he's a lucky guy.'

Maree remembered her conversation with Tom on Saturday morning at his house. That's what he'd meant when he said she had nothing to worry about from him seeing her naked, or about not wanting to take advantage of her.

She felt let down. Was she feeling disappointed that Tom was gay? She wasn't interested in him. She would never date an actor.

'Next time I'll get him to give me a lift home,' Emma said. 'A romance between the lead actors always leads to more publicity.'

Maree felt used. Now she knew why Tom had insisted on driving her home. Photos like this one wouldn't hurt his reputation. All this time she'd thought he was being nice to her because he was attracted onto her, now she realized it was an elaborate charade to help maintain his straight persona.

'This looks great.' Emma rubbed her hip. 'I love it.'

'Thanks.' Maree forced a smile. 'You make it work.'

Emma smiled back at her, and went to change out of the costume. 'See you on set,' she said after she exited the change room a little while later, dressed in her regular clothes again.

Maree nodded. Shooting started in a week.

There was a knock at the door and Emma opened it.

'Hello,' she said as Tom entered. 'I'll see you on set.' Emma walked by with none of her usual flirting. She wasn't going to waste her time on a guy who didn't appreciate her charms.

Tom looked bemused for a moment before turning to Maree. 'How are you feeling?'

'Fine.' She handed him his outfit and pointed him in the direction of the change room.

When he returned dressed in his costume, she spoke curtly. 'Stand here.' She pointed to the stool.

'Is everything okay?' Tom asked.

'Fine.' Maree knelt on the floor and started hemming his pants.

'Did I do something wrong?'

She stood and went to get her cell phone. She tapped on the screen until she found the photo and handed it to him.

'It could have been worse.' Tom handed her the phone back.

'Could it? Because I usually make it a point not to be in the tabloids at all.' Maree kneeled down again and resumed pinning. She stabbed a pin through the pant leg and straight into her index finger. 'Ouch,' she muttered and sucked on it as she stood up. 'Finished.'

Tom stepped into the change room. 'I'm sorry,' he said through the curtain. 'This photographer has been stalking me for a year now. He's on my tail everywhere I go.'

Maree rifled through her desk for a band aid. 'And I'm sure you don't mind the pics he publishes to help your playboy reputation.'

'Actually, yes, I do mind, but it's not like I can do anything about it.'

Tom was sounding frustrated, but Maree didn't care. He didn't deserve any sympathy. He chose to be an actor and he had to live with the consequences, but she didn't. She purposely remained out of the limelight so she didn't have to deal with crap like this. 'This is why I don't date actors,' she said.

Tom came out of the change room in his jeans and T-shirt and saw her struggling to open the band aid with her sore finger.

'Here, let me help.' He took the band aid from her and tore open the packaging. He peeled the plastic tabs and held the band aid out for her. Maree placed her finger on the soft pad. As he gently pressed down the adhesive she was aware of how close they were. His chest was bumping her elbow. As she breathed in she smelled his aftershave and felt tendrils of attraction unfurl in her stomach.

'I had no choice but to get you out of the club,' Tom said.

She met his gaze, trying to remember the conversation thread. 'You could have left me. Allegra would have taken care of me if I was drunk.' Usually Maree was the designated driver and Allegra could get crazy drunk, secure in the knowledge that Maree would make sure she got home safe. She couldn't imagine that Allegra would have toned down her behavior at her own birthday party.

'Allegra was too busy partying to notice you were sucking face with Leather Pants,' Tom snapped.

Maree gasped as her memories came flooding back. She remembered that she came onto Tom, but he'd gently rejected her. She'd been embarrassed and hurt. Steve—Leather Pants man—saw her and asked her what was wrong. He took her to the couch and after a few minutes of conversation he'd kissed her. She had known that by letting him kiss her she was giving him the signal that she wanted more, but she'd been feeling so lonely and hurt, all she wanted was a distraction to take the pain away.

Then Tom had shown up and, seeing the shock on his face, Maree had realized what she was doing. She'd regressed back to her party-girl persona, where all she wanted was a boy to give her attention and soothe the pain. Tom offered to take her home, and she'd accepted.

'But why didn't you take me to my place?' she asked.

'The paparazzo was following us. I didn't want him to have your address. And then when I had to stop the car while you vomited I made a deal with him so he didn't photograph you.'

'A deal?'

'I went surfing yesterday and he got the exclusive.'

When she was scrolling through the pics on Emma's phone Maree had seen the shots of Tom in swimming trunks holding a surfboard as he peered out to the ocean. The photos were too sharp and clear to be random paparazzi photos taken from a distance, and she'd immediately known that Tom was fully aware of the photographer's presence. She'd taken this as yet another piece of evidence that he was a vain actor always looking for attention.

Maree felt small and embarrassed. She couldn't believe she'd been so wrong about him. She'd interpreted his every gesture with suspicion, seeing underhanded motivations when there were none. What was wrong with her? While she'd always been wary around actors, she'd never been so close-minded in her life. Was Allegra right, and Beau had broken something inside of her?

'I'm sorry,' said Maree.

Tom shrugged it off, but she could see the hurt on his face.

'Why are you so nice to me?' she asked.

'Why wouldn't I be nice to you?'

As they gazed into each other's eyes he looked like a man who had kissing on his mind. Maree didn't know what to do. She didn't know if she wanted to kiss him, but she was also scared that if she turned away again, she might make a fool of herself. What if he didn't want to kiss her at all and she was imagining it?

There was a knock on the door and it opened. A man entered, his brown hair and eyes a match to Maree's. Someone might mistake them for siblings because his unlined face made him look younger than he was, but when they looked closer they would realize that the unmoving, opaque skin was the result of medical intervention. Her father was not someone who welcomed the tell-tale signs of aging.

Tom stepped back. Maree would have been relieved by the interruption if it was anyone else.

Chapter 12

'Darling Maree.' He came in, but instead of going to Maree's side he went straight up to Tom. 'Are you going to introduce me to your boyfriend?'

'This is not my boyfriend,' Maree said through gritted teeth. 'This is my colleague, Tom Calvert. Tom, meet my father, John Reynard.'

'It's nice to meet you.' John shook Tom's hand. 'I'm so glad my daughter has made a new friend.' John put special emphasis on the word 'friend.'

Maree's hands were clenched into fists. She'd told Beau that her relationship with her father was strained, but since Tom didn't know that, he had to act oblivious.

'Nice to meet you, too,' Tom said.

'I'm very happy that you got the lead in *Ten Steps*. Robert has been trying to get the script developed for years,' John said, referring to the director. 'He was considering me for the lead a few years ago.'

'Don't you mean a few decades ago,' Maree interrupted. 'After all, you turned sixty—'

'I couldn't do it, of course,' John continued as if Maree hadn't spoken. 'The movie clashed with my schedule for *The Valiant and the Vain.'* The soap opera had been on television screens for decades and was one of the only television shows still in production that had started out in black and white. 'Just as well the movie didn't happen back then. Now Robert can do it justice with all the special effects we have access to these days. So when does shooting start?'

Tom left a pause for Maree to speak up, but she was looking mutinously at the floor.

'Next week. I'm just finalizing the fittings.' Tom smiled. 'You must be proud of Maree. She's doing a fantastic job on the costumes.'

'Of course,' John said. 'At least she's still in the business, as we say. My younger daughter, Jennifer, is following in her dad's footsteps.' John took out his cell phone and scrolled down, showing Tom photos of a leggy blonde. 'She's had guest roles in CSI and Law & Order, and she's auditioning for her first supporting role in a Tom Cruise movie. She's a real beauty.'

'Well it must be wonderful to have two talented daughters,' Tom said.

'Of course.' John nodded. 'Maybe you'll get the chance to work with my Jennifer soon.'

He was acutely aware of the hurt on Maree's face. 'It was nice to meet you,' Tom said. The only thing he could do for Maree was leave so she wasn't embarrassed any further by her father.

'I came to invite my daughter out to lunch. Would you like to join us?' John asked.

'No, thank you.' Tom walked toward the door. 'I have to get going.'

'Perhaps another time,' John quickly added. 'Maree can bring you to a family dinner and you can meet Jennifer.'

Tom stopped at the door. Maree's face was flushed with embarrassment. 'That's up to Maree. See you.'

He walked out to the parking lot, and hunted through his pockets for his keys. He must have left them in Maree's office. He leaned against the car and waited for Maree and her father to leave for lunch. Then he could return to her office and find his keys. Five minutes later Maree walked toward him.

'I think you forgot these.' She held out his keys.

'Thanks. I was going to wait for you and your dad to leave before I returned.'

'No need. He lost interest in having lunch with me the minute you left.'

Tom nodded.

'I'm sorry about him.'

'You don't need to apologize. That's on him, it's not on you.' He took her hand and gently squeezed it.

Maree quickly looked away. 'I haven't seen him in six months, you know.' She said it softly. 'And then the morning that I'm in the tabloids with a movie star he suddenly wants to have lunch with me.'

Tom didn't say anything, just held her hand. They were in that sort of industry where someone always wanted a piece of them, still, when it was your family it would be so much worse.

She shrugged. 'It seems all I do is apologize to you.'

'Then don't.'

She looked taken aback.

'There's nothing you need to apologize for.'

'I don't know about that.'

'I do.' Tom stepped back. 'Have you had lunch?'

Maree shook her head.

'Do you want to join me?'

She looked undecided.

'I'm just asking you to go to lunch as friends.'

'Is that what we are? Friends?' Maree asked.

'It's what I'd like us to be.'

She scanned his eyes for intention. 'Are you sure? Because usually when a man and a woman are friends it's because one of them is interested, but the other isn't.'

'Does that mean that you're interested in me?' he asked.

'No, no, that's not what I'm saying.' Maree was flustered. 'I just don't know if a man and a woman can be friends without ...'

'I don't know either,' Tom said. 'But what I do know is that I'm not in a position to offer you anything more right now. Can't we just get to know each other and see what happens?'

He was sick of manipulating and trying to force things. He wanted to be as honest as he could, and right now all he wanted was for them to get to know each other; for Maree to stop putting up her guard and for him to have the chance to tell her the truth, and he couldn't do that if she was always so defensive around him.

Maree nodded slowly. 'Okay, friends it is.'

He opened the passenger door for her. As she sat down he smelled her perfume and felt a flash of desire. He closed the door again. *You're friends only.*

'What happened with the note from the stalker?' Maree asked when he climbed into the driver's seat.

'We've given the note to the police so the ball is in their court.' The letter had been a rambling diatribe about the way that he used people and discarded them when he was done. It had finished with a warning that what goes around, comes around.

'You sound like you're worried.'

He looked at her with surprise. He'd deliberately tried to keep his voice neutral so she wouldn't know how bothered he was. He didn't want her to have one more strike against dating him.

'I just feel like the police are being a bit too blasé about the whole thing,' Tom said. He'd read an implicit threat in the letter. It was almost like the stalker knew him and believed he'd done them wrong, but the police were unconvinced. They just thought that the stalker was using a cliché.

'They probably are. Most times they assume that the celebrity is just trying to drum up publicity.'

'You sound like you agree with them.' Tom put on his indicator and turned out of the parking lot.

'Sometimes the police are right, but that doesn't seem to be the case with you. You might need to be more proactive.'

He felt relief that she didn't think he was a publicity chaser. Maybe she was warming to him.

Tom parked the car and came around the car to open the door for her. As they walked up to the pizza restaurant Maree looked around in surprise.

'Something wrong?' he asked.

'I wasn't expecting this,' she said, as he opened the door and they stepped in.

The pizzeria was a local, family-owned business with timber-panelled walls and a wood-fired oven at the back. Tom had discovered it years ago and it was one of his favorite eateries.

'What were you expecting?'

'Something shiny, swanky and modern where cocktails are served by lovely women in slinky dresses.'

'Ouch,' Tom said. 'Maybe you don't know me as well as you think.'

Maree smiled. 'Maybe.'

'Tommy!' A man with an Elvis hairstyle and flashing teeth met them at the door. 'It's been ages.'

'Hello, Carlo,' Tom said with a smile. 'It's been a crazy few months.'

'And who is your friend?' Carlo asked as he showed them to a table.

'Maree is the costume designer on the movie I'm shooting,' Tom said after he'd performed introductions. 'So how is the family?'

'The twins are sophomores at high school.'

'Wow, that's quick. I remember them running around here in pigtails.'

'I'm terrified. With big kids come big problems.'

'They're good girls,' Tom assured him. 'How is Linda?'

'She's at home resting. The new bambino is very big.' Carlo held his hands out in front of his stomach.

'She's pregnant?' Tom asked.

Carlo nodded with a smile.

Tom stood and hugged him. 'I'm so happy for you.'

Carlo teared up. 'The Lord has blessed us after all these years.'

The bell rang and Carlo looked up. A group of men in business suits entered.

'You'll have to tell me about the new movie later. What would you like to drink?' Carlo took their orders and returned to the front.

'You've known each other a long time?' Maree asked, her expression quizzical.

'This was my first job when I came to LA all those years ago,' Tom said.

'Really?' Maree looked around with interest.

'That's right. I was the delivery driver. It was the perfect gig so I could make auditions during the day.'

'Who would have thought?' Maree said with a smile.

Carlo returned with their drinks and they placed their orders.

'So is it just me or do you think badly of all actors?' Tom asked.

'Can you blame me?' Maree said.

'But you've been in the business for years. You know not all actors are shady.'

'Of course,' Maree said. 'But I like to maintain a professional distance from my coworkers.' She looked up when she realized how abrupt that sounded. 'Present company excluded of course.'

'So I'm becoming the exception to the rule?' Tom asked.

'Maybe.' Maree twirled her straw, making the ice cubes tinkle as they hit the side of the glass.

'So, you and your father are not close?' Tom asked. Even though she'd shared some details with Beau, he was curious about the simmering tension between them.

Maree shook her head. 'My parents divorced when I was one and my dad remarried soon after. I hardly saw him until my mom died of cancer when I was eight years old and I had to go live with him, but I never felt like a part of the family. My dad didn't really want me around spoiling his new family.'

'And you're not close to your sister either?'

Maree's lips curled into a semblance of a smile. 'Just think of me as Cinderella who had to endure the typical wicked stepmother and half-sister.' Her voice was tight with pent-up emotion. 'As soon as I was eighteen years old I got out of there and moved back into the house my mother left me. Thankfully she'd written an air-tight will so my father couldn't sell it. I've been on my own ever since.'

'I'm sorry.'

Maree shrugged. 'You can't choose your family, right?'

Their pizzas were delivered to their table, steam rising from the crust.

Maree took a slice and bit in. 'This is delicious.' She closed her eyes, a look of ecstasy on her face as she chewed.

Tom shifted in his seat. *Friends, friends*, he chanted to himself.

'Where are you from?'

'Jackson City, Tennessee.' Tom was relieved that Beau didn't share the name of his hometown, leaving him free to tell the truth. 'It was my dream to be an actor, but Dad wanted me to be an engineer. I lasted one semester at college before dropping out and getting on a bus to LA.'

'And the rest is history.' Maree smiled, her eyes sparkling.

For the first time she was being the Maree that he knew with Tom. She was letting her guard down and letting him in.

'That's right,' Tom said. 'We'll just skip over all the years of crap jobs, no money, and the revolving door of failed auditions, and jump straight to the success story.'

'Your parents must be happy.' Maree was nibbling on her pizza crust.

Tom shook his head. 'Dad keeps asking when I'll get a real job, and Mom wants to know when I'll settle down with a nice girl.'

Maree laughed. 'Is there any such thing as a nice girl or boy in this town?'

'I think you're a nice girl,' Tom said.

Maree snatched the pizza crust off his plate. 'I'm not that nice.'

He laughed as she ate his crust.

'What about you? You just went through a bad break up?'

Maree sighed. 'Yes.'

'What happened?'

Sadness shadowed her face.

'Sorry, I didn't meant to pry,' Tom said, angry with himself for bringing it up.

'No, it's okay. I met someone and I thought he was the real deal, but he turned out to be a liar. He didn't even have the guts to tell me to my face and instead confessed in a Dear Jane letter before disappearing forever. It seems to be the story of my life. I meet men who always turn out to be something else.'

'I'm sorry.'

'Don't be.' She smiled. 'It's not as if it's your fault.'

Tom looked at the table. He'd never felt so small in his life.

'What about you? You said that you lost someone because of your arrogance,' Maree asked.

Tom hesitated, searching for words so that he was telling the truth. 'I took her for granted and didn't realize she was special until it was too late,' he finally said.

'Did you try to get her back?' Maree tilted her head as she waited for him to answer.

Tom hesitated, lost for words. Thankfully Carlo saved him from answering when he offered them the dessert menu. By the time they placed their orders their conversation turned away from the serious and they talked about people they knew in the industry.

After Tom paid the check and they'd farewelled Carlo, he drove her back to the studio and parked the car.

'Thanks for lunch,' Maree said as he helped her out of the car.

'You're welcome.'

'I had a great time.'

'You say that like you're surprised,' Tom said.

Maree laughed. 'I guess I am.'

'I don't know whether to be flattered or insulted.' He leaned against the car.

'Flattered. Definitely flattered.'

Her face was lifted toward his and he felt desire stir in his gut. All he had to do was bend down and their lips would touch. She was so close that when the breeze lifted tendrils of her hair they brushed his face. The world slowed as the moment stretched out. He bent his head. He heard her take a breath, and her eyes fluttered closed. He hesitated, his lips a whisper breath from hers. Then he moved to kiss her cheek.

Maree opened her eyes and looked at him in confusion.

He hesitated, wanting to say something, but not knowing what. In the end he nodded and got in the car. He watched her walk to the studio.

'Dammit,' he shouted as he gripped the steering wheel.

He turned on the ignition and drove toward town to meet with Carter. The lunch date had gone better than he could have imagined. He was finally connecting with Maree, and had felt hopeful that his plan to win her over was working, and yet when the moment came to kiss her he couldn't do it.

Carter was in his office, his desk strewn with paper as he stared at his screen.

'You're late,' Carter said as Tom entered and sat on the sofa in front of his desk.

'Sorry.' Tom had sent him a text message. 'I had lunch with Maree.'

'And how is your grand reunion going?' Carter he leaned back in his chair.

'Great.' Tom frowned as he traced the lines on his palm with his finger. That niggling feeling he'd had when he dropped Maree off was still with him.

'Are you sure?'

'She's finally relaxing with me and we had a great connection.' Why was it that when he had everything he wanted, he was feeling so lousy?

'That means your plan is working. She's on her way to falling for Tom Calvert.'

Tom stood and started pacing. 'Yes.'

He should have felt ecstatic that things were progressing so well, but all he felt was this sense of wrongness.

'She means a lot to you,' Carter said, watching him.

'She means everything.'

Losing her as Beau had made him realize how much he cared about her and how empty his life was without her. That's why he'd been determined to do whatever it would take to get her back in his life. But now Tom wondered if the price was going to be too high.

Carter looked closer at him. 'I've never seen you like this before, and we've known each other for what, six years?'

'That's because I hadn't met Maree,' Tom said. 'And we've known each other for nine years.'

'Nine years?' Carter repeated questioningly. 'Are you sure?'

Tom just looked at him.

'Okay, nine years.'

'I don't want to lie to her, but I don't know what to do.' Tom leaned against the window and stared out at the view of the Los Angeles skyline.

'There's only one thing you can do.'

Tom nodded. He had to tell her the truth. He'd had this hope that if she had time to get to know him as Tom she would find it easier to accept what he'd done as Beau. But now he knew that the longer he lied to her, the worse it was going to be when he finally confessed.

'But what if she won't want to work on the movie once she knows?' Tom's biggest fear was that she would want nothing to do with him, that she wouldn't be able to work in such close proximity to him. 'She'll lose her chance at her dream.'

'Not your problem. All you can do is tell her the truth and let her decide what to do with it.'

Tom knew that Carter's focus was only on his career. Carter was worried that with Maree as a distraction he wouldn't be able to focus on Ten Steps. Still, that didn't mean Carter wasn't right about telling her the truth. The longer Tom waited to tell her, the worse it would be. If he just told her now it would be like ripping off a band aid—painful in the short term, but better in the long term.

'You're right.' He felt relieved as he made his decision. While he was scared of what might happen, he also couldn't wait to leave this burden of guilt behind. 'I'm going to tell her.'

'Good. Glad that's resolved.' Carter slapped his hands together. 'Now we need to move onto your secret admirer.'

'What did the police say?'

When Maree handed him the white envelope on Sunday morning, he knew instantly what it was. He'd been receiving love letters from a stalker for nearly a year. At first he didn't think much of it, but when the letters kept arriving even when he was overseas on location, he'd realized that his secret admirer was taking a very close interest in his comings and goings.

After he'd dropped Maree home, he'd gone to Carter and they went to the police together with the envelope. Tom had made a statement and Carter said he'd follow up.

'They're investigating,' Carter said now.

'But?' Tom asked.

'But it's not going to be a priority for them. After all, this stalker seems benign from their point of view. She's just sending a few letters and being overly concerned with your career. There are no threats to your safety or anything.'

The letters were typed and printed on white paper, with no identifying features. They seemed to be the ramblings of a fan—warning him about the consequences of his partying lifestyle. However, Tom was beginning to think this stalker was anything but benign.

'What about Betty?' Tom asked, referring to Carter's dog.

Carter had had to take a trip out of town and his usual dogsitter had fallen through, so Tom had volunteered to look after Betty. He liked dogs, but he'd never been able to get one; his erratic lifestyle wouldn't be fair on a pet. One day into her stay with him she went missing from his backyard.

She was found in a ravine, her throat slashed. Tom had already received a few letters from the stalker by then, but hadn't made any connection—until a letter arrived after Betty was killed, warning him to keep focused on his career and not let distractions get in the way.

Tom still didn't think too much of it, but Carter insisted they bring it to the attention of the police. Carter was convinced the stalker killed Betty because she thought Tom had adopted a dog. The police didn't agree with his theory and still considered the stalker low priority, but Tom was beginning to come around to Carter's point of view. The stalker knew too much and was able to follow his movements a little too closely for comfort. This suggested an obsessive nature.

He was getting scared that the stalker was working up to something bigger, and now that he had Maree in his life he really had something to lose. If the stalker had killed a dog because she thought it would take his attention away from his career, what would she do to Maree?

'The police still don't believe that Betty was killed by the stalker,' Carter said. 'Their theory is that it was a young kid in the area. They found other animal carcasses nearby with similar wounds.'

'But you don't agree?' Tom said.

'No.' Carter shook his head. 'The M.O. with Betty was different. There was a frenzy that suggests loss of control. I think your stalker was acting out of a jealous rage.'

'Did the police question Norman Keller?'

Tom had given the police his name as a possible witness in case Norman had followed him home and seen anything. Plus he'd had the idea that perhaps the photographer and the stalker could be one and the same. Norman also had an uncanny knack of tracing Tom's whereabouts.

'He was at home sending the photos he took of you and Maree to his editor,' Carter said. 'The police tracked his emails to confirm it.'

Tom rubbed his neck. He'd been hoping that Norman was involved so he could put this whole mess to bed, but now it seemed he was no closer to finding out who his stalker was. A thought occurred to him.

'What if she saw me with Maree today?' He kept seeing the photo of Betty that Carter had shown him. For someone to kill a poor defenseless dog made his blood run cold at their level of ruthlessness.

'You know my advice,' Carter said.

'I'm not getting a bodyguard.'

He hated the thought of his privacy being compromised in that way. Not to mention that the tabloids would have a feeding frenzy, giving the stalker publicity, which was the last thing they needed right now. So far Tom had managed to keep it off the radar and he wanted it to stay that way. While some celebrities might enjoy the media attention that came with a story like this, Tom had had enough of making the tabloid rounds for all the wrong reasons.

In the past two years, since he'd been charged over the cocaine possession, he'd been a tabloid favorite. The paparazzi purposely tried to incite him. They'd followed him for months, waiting for another slip up, but Tom had realized he was a step away from crossing to the dark side of Hollywood celebrity and becoming a has-been. Since then he'd cleaned up his act—avoided the clubs, the serial dating and the party scene. The paparazzi had backed off, finding the lack of extracurricular activity boring. And Tom wanted to keep it that way.

'Then there's only one other thing we can do,' Carter said. 'We'll have to hire you an investigator, someone who can find out who this nut is and keep tabs on her. Once we know who she is and have proof that she's breaking the law we might have something concrete we can take to the police.'

'Okay, do it,' Tom said. 'Just make sure it's someone discreet. I don't want to see this anywhere.'

'Will do,' Carter said.

Chapter 13

Maree waved when she spotted Allegra. She'd been waiting for fifteen minutes and as usual Allegra was late.

'Sorry,' Allegra was breathing heavily. At least she had the decency to hurry now. 'My date dropped me off and we were in the parking lot making out for a while.'

Maree sighed. She should have known it was too good to be true that Allegra was puffed out from rushing.

Allegra took a sip of the coffee that Maree had ordered for her and screwed up her face in disgust. 'That's cold.'

'It was hot fifteen minutes ago.'

Allegra looked chastened. 'Sorry, but honestly how could I resist?' She held up her phone and showed Maree a pic of her new man. 'Look at that dreamy smile.'

Maree rolled her eyes. Allegra always had to have a warm body on the go.

'So give me all the sordid details about you and Tom Calvert,' Allegra said, after she put down her phone.

'There are no sordid details,' Maree said.

'Really? So he just took you home from the club on Saturday and nothing happened?'

Maree maintained eye contact even though she felt her face flush. 'That's right, nothing happened.'

Allegra narrowed her eyes. 'You're flushed. That means you're fibbing.' She tilted her head to the right. 'But you're able to maintain eye contact which means that you're telling the truth that nothing happened, so I'm guessing you're fibbing about something.'

'All right, all right.' Maree gave in. Allegra was like a sniffer dog when she sensed a story. 'He took me back to his place.'

'He did?' Allegra squeezed her arm. 'What was he like? Did he have a lot of stamina?'

'No, I told you, nothing happened.'

'Really?' Allegra's voice changed and took on a monotone. 'You went home with a hottie like Tom Calvert and nothing happened?'

'No, I mean yes. That's what I'm saying. Nothing happened.' Maree said. 'I got sick on the way home and he took me to his place, helped me shower and change, and let me sleep.'

'So you slept alone in his bed?' Allegra was sitting up straight, her face screwed up in a quizzical expression.

'Well, no, in his guest bedroom actually.'

Allegra gave a sigh and stirred her cold coffee with the spoon. 'Typical. All the good ones are gay.'

'You think he's gay?' Maree asked.

'I didn't until now.'

'But I'd vomited and was really sick. Maybe he was just being considerate by letting me rest.'

'Then he should have taken you home.'

'He said a photographer was following us and he didn't want him to find out where I lived.'

'When exactly did he say that?' Allegra asked.

'The next day in my office.'

'You haven't seen him since?'

'We had lunch yesterday.'

'Maybe I'm wrong. If he invited you to lunch, then maybe he isn't gay.' Allegra straightened up and smiled. 'This is great. It's just what you need—a rebound guy. Someone hot you can have some fun with, but not take seriously while you get over what's his face.' Allegra paused, looking at Maree's expression. 'What's the matter?'

'Well, he didn't actually ask me out,' she said. 'We had a fitting appointment and my dad showed up.'

Allegra's smile faded. 'What did Plastic Face want?'

Allegra knew her father and she wasn't impressed with him. Over the years she had witnessed the hundreds of let downs and put downs he'd subjected Maree to.

'He saw the photo of me in the tabloids.'

Allegra shook her head. 'That man is a vampire. Now that he thinks you're hobnobbing with movie stars he wants to know you.'

Maree gave a faint nod.

When she told Tom that her upbringing was a Cinderella story she hadn't been straying too far from the truth. Her father had remarried soon after her mother passed away and Maree went to live with him. Her stepmother had been a benign if cold presence for the first few years, but when Jennifer was born she changed, and began to regard Maree as an intruder into her perfect family.

When her father proposed Maree come to the studio with him during summer vacation to give her stepmother some peace and quiet, Maree had been full of excitement. She'd thought she'd finally have the chance to forge a relationship with her father away from her stepmother's influence. She'd been wrong.

Her father left her to her own devices. She'd met Mack and the studio lot became their playground. Some days she only saw her father in the car when they were driving back and forth from home. She and Mack became inseparable and soon she'd spent most weekends at his house, which became like her second home.

'Now you've got even more reason to go out with Tom,' Allegra said. 'Let your daddy and his Stepford family eat their hearts out.'

Her stepmother and half-sister were even bigger social climbers than her father—they had probably sent him yesterday to try to ingratiate himself again. In her heart of hearts Maree was tempted. The thought of their envy if she was photographed again with Tom would be so delicious.

'When are you seeing Tom again?'

'Next week when we start shooting.' Maree drank the last of her coffee. 'And we're not dating. He just wants to be friends.'

Even though she was telling the truth she felt a surge of disappointment. She remembered yesterday when Tom had dropped her off. There had been a moment when she'd wanted him to kiss her. She hadn't realized that he'd gotten under her skin, but sometime during their lunch together something had clicked and she'd felt a sense of deja vu. There was something about Tom that made her feel like they were two souls who had lived a previous life together.

'Oh, God. He is gay!' Allegra threw her spoon on the table and it landed with a clatter. 'Screw him. We'll find someone else. What did you think of Steve?'

Maree's mind flashed back to the club and kissing Leather Pants, AKA Steve. Every time she thought of it she felt a curdle of shame settle in her gut.

'No, not him.'

'Leave it with me. I'll find someone by the end of the day.'

'I'm not ready to date,' Maree said. Allegra was as good as her word and would go through her contacts to find what she viewed as the 'perfect' date. He might even be one of her former lovers. Allegra was all about recycling.

'Not going to happen. You've been acting like you're in mourning for the past two months. It's time for living.'

Even though Maree agreed with Allegra and knew it was time for her to get on with her life, she wasn't sure that random dating was quite what she had in mind.

Maree's phone beeped and she picked it up. She was surprised to see the name appearing on the screen.

'Who is it?' Allegra asked. She took the phone from Maree and saw Tom's name. 'Interesting.' She pressed the answer button and passed it back.

Maree quickly snatched the phone. She felt caught off guard. She hadn't been sure she would take the call, but now Allegra had forced her.

'Hello,' she said breathlessly.

'Maree, it's Tom.' His deep voice filled her ear. She felt a thrill in her stomach. 'I was wondering if you were available for lunch today?'

'Lunch?' Maree repeated, stalling for time.

Allegra threw her napkin at her. 'Yes, yes,' she mouthed.

Maree gave a sigh. If she tried to evade, Allegra would snatch the phone off her again and arrange the date for her.

'Yes, I'm available.'

'Great, I'll pick you up at one o'clock,' Tom said. 'See you then.'

Maree hung up, still staring at the phone. Why did he call her already? If they were dating she would have expected a follow-up call the next day, but considering they were supposed to be just friends she wasn't sure how to take it.

'That was promising.' Allegra was smiling like the cat who got the cream. 'Maybe he isn't gay after all.'

'Maybe I don't care.' Maree threw her phone on the table in frustration. 'Maybe I'm sick of games and not knowing where I stand.'

'Good, there's the fire,' said Allegra. 'There's only one thing to do—you just need to plant one on him and you'll know.'

'I already did,' Maree said. 'I tried to kiss him at the club.'

'And?'

'He wasn't into it.'

Allegra clutched her head and groaned so loudly that everyone in the café turned to look at her. 'Where do you meet these guys?' she demanded.

Maree started laughing and she couldn't stop. Trust Allegra to get to the heart of the matter. Beau had left her confused, and being with Tom was like being on spin cycle. She didn't know which way she was coming or going. 'I don't know.'

'Well, if he doesn't kiss you tomorrow, you cut him off. You have enough friends. What you need is a hot lover who will make you forget what's his name.'

Maree smiled. 'Thanks.'

Everything was clear after talking to Allegra. She had to admit she was attracted to Tom, but if he didn't feel the same way, she had to put a stop to their 'friends game.' She was too emotionally fragile to be in a one-sided attraction.

Maree realized something had changed inside of her. While she was still hurt by Beau, and she didn't think she would ever get over that betrayal, she was ready to move forward. There were some things she knew she wanted out of life, namely a partner and children. And the only way she was going to make them happen was by opening her heart to love again.

She knew she would be more cautious with love in the future. She wouldn't ever be able to rush in the way she did with Beau, but she was sure there was someone out there for her. Someone who was right for her and could fill the empty spaces inside.

'You're right,' she told Allegra.

'I am?' Allegra sat up. 'What am I right about?'

'If Tom isn't into me, then I need to stop seeing him. It's time for me to get out there.'

'Yes, yes,' Allegra lifted her fisted hands in the air. 'That's what I want to hear. If you don't have a date on Friday night then you and I are going on the prowl.'

'All right,' Maree said. 'I'll drive.'

In her role as designated driver she would have to remain sober and could ensure she didn't make the same mistake. She felt a sense of peace that had been missing in her life since she met Beau. Allegra was right. It was time for living.

·❤·❤·❤·❤·❤·

The morning passed in a heightened sense of anticipation as Maree waited for Tom. Even though she was busy, she was aware of the ticking clock and the minutes passing until he arrived.

When she heard a knock on the door she straightened from the mannequin she had been fitting. Tom opened the door and stepped in. Warmth hit her stomach as she noticed the way his T-shirt curved around his biceps and chest.

Maree walked over and kissed him on the cheek. He kissed her back, his lips barely grazing her skin. He walked away from her and admired the costume on the mannequin.

She was creating Rex's outfit for the judgment scene. She'd removed the color panels and made the tunic monochrome. 'What do you think?'

Tom walked around the mannequin and nodded. 'This is great.'

'Not *Tour de France*,' she teased, reminding him of his critique when he saw her sketch for the first time.

Tom forced a smile. 'No. This is perfect.'

She was confused that he was so distant.

'Ready to go?' he asked.

She nodded and got her handbag. 'Where are we going?'

'Wherever you like.' He shrugged.

'Okay.'

Tom drove while Maree gave him directions. She tried making conversation, asking him about his day and rehearsals, but he'd answer and let the conversation peter out.

Butterflies fluttered in her stomach. She'd decided that she had to be up front with him and find out once and for all how he felt about her, but the nerves were now kicking in. How exactly do you ask a guy if he's into you? When he'd first arrived she was sure he was, but now he had a preoccupied air that was giving her pause.

Maree indicated where to park, then led him around the corner to the restaurant. The restaurant was in a Spanish-style home with only a discreet sign above the doorway identifying it. As Tom opened the door for her she walked past him and smelled his aftershave.

The interior was bathed from the sunlight pouring through the windows. The walls were covered with photos and the wooden tables and chairs were an eclectic mix, creating a homey atmosphere. This was Maree's favorite Mexican restaurant; she and Mack used to hang out here when she was young, and it was still owned by the same family.

'I was surprised to get your phone call this morning,' Maree said as Tom held out the chair for her.

He quirked an eyebrow as he took a seat across from her.

'We only had lunch yesterday and here we are again.'

'That's right.' Tom rubbed the back of his neck as the silence stretched out.

'It's almost as if you can't get enough of me.' Maree laughed nervously and picked up the menu.

She'd meant that line to come off as light-hearted and funny, a way of opening up the conversation about Tom's feelings for her, but seeing the frown on his face her stomach tightened with nerves.

After the waiter left with their drink order Maree looked at the menu for a distraction, peering at Tom over the top. He was staring at the print, his eyes not moving. She couldn't take the tension anymore.

'Is something wrong?' she asked.

'No. Nothing's wrong.'

'Really? Because you're certainly behaving like something's wrong.' She was getting irritated at his monosyllabic answers. He was acting like he wanted to be anywhere but here, yet he was the one who'd asked her out.

There was a long pause as Tom looked undecided. The waiter arrived and served their drinks. After he left them alone again, Maree bit her lip to stop herself from jumping in and smoothing the awkward tension.

Finally Tom took a deep breath. 'There's something I have to tell you.' He kept his eyes on the table, as though he couldn't look at her face. 'I've enjoyed spending time with you these past few days.'

Her stomach lurched as she recognized the opening line of a breakup speech. How could he be breaking up with her, they weren't even going out? They were just friends. She thought she'd plumbed the depths of humiliation on Friday night when she'd vomited in front of him, this was a whole new level.

'I should have told you from the start, but I was hoping that if you got to know me—'

The penny dropped and she felt like such a fool. 'I knew it,' Maree muttered, feeling angry with herself. She should have trusted her instincts from the get-go, instead she'd let him under her guard. She threw her menu on the table and stood. 'Why do I keep doing this to myself? Why do I keep falling for guys who are liars?'

'Please Maree, let me finish.' Tom got up and took her hand.

She shook him off. 'There's no need,' Maree snapped. 'I know exactly where this conversation is going and I don't want to hear any more. You're gay. I don't need you to say it.'

'What?' Tom exclaimed, his face shocked. 'I'm not gay.'

'You're not?' Maree put her hand on her hip and looked at him.

'No, of course not.' Tom shook his head. 'Why would you think that?'

'I don't know. Maybe because you want to be friends'

'That doesn't make me gay.'

'No, I guess not. But you didn't want to kiss me.'

'I'm not gay.'

She stared at him, the humiliation of her two rebuffed attempts washed over her again. She'd never had a guy turn away from her like that. She was so confused. Every time she saw him things just got murkier and harder to bear. Should it be this hard? Usually boy meets girl. Boy likes girl. Girl likes boy. End of story.

'Don't worry about it. This is not working.' Maree pushed her chair behind the table. 'This 'friends' experiment is over. From now on we're coworkers and nothing more.'

Maree picked up her handbag and headed out the door.

'No, wait, Maree.'

She heard him fumbling with his wallet behind her to pay for their drinks, but she didn't turn around. For the first time in months she felt strong. Allegra had been telling her for years that she let men walk all over her. That they got what they needed and left her behind, but she hadn't believed it. She'd thought all her exes were nice guys and the timing was wrong, but she had to face the truth. Maree was always the loser in the relationships. It was time she changed her story.

She heard footsteps behind her and Tom grabbed her arm and turned her around.

'Maree, it's not true that I don't want to kiss you.' His face was laid bare and there was torment in his eyes. 'I wanted to kiss you on Saturday at the club and I wanted to kiss you yesterday and I want to kiss you now. It's all I think about.' His voice was raspy with need.

They were so close she felt his breath on her face. 'So why didn't you?' Maree asked.

His face was pained as he stared at her mouth. It was as if he was desperate to kiss her, but there was something stopping him.

Maree sighed and went to pull away, but he drew her closer and wrapped his arms around her, cupping her head, as he leaned down to kiss her. She stiffened, the sudden body contact shocking her. She put her hands on his chest to push him away. How dare her touch her after everything he'd put her through?

Tom's kiss was passionate and urgent, as if he felt at any moment that she would disappear. She melted into him. Something about his kiss transported her, it felt so dangerous and yet so familiar. It was like they had kissed before in another life.

A beeping intruded into her consciousness. Tom lifted his head. His face was softened, his eyes glowing with desire.

'It's my car alarm,' Tom whispered. 'Stay here. I'll be right back, we need to talk.'

Maree nodded, feeling dazed. She watched him walk away, her whole body alive. What had just happened? One minute she thought he wasn't into her, that she never wanted to see him again, the next her whole body was aching with need. She was shaken by the depth of her want.

Tom turned to look over her shoulder, as if he needed to make sure she was still there.

She heard a car driving down the street, the motor thrumming, but didn't pay any mind. Tom's expression changed to a look of fear. He opened his mouth, forming her name.

She turned her head and looked. The car was driving down the wrong side of the street, and it jumped the curb and headed for her. In the two seconds it took her brain to process what was happening, the car was nearly on top of her. She started to run.

Chapter 14

Tom was crossing the street, feeling on top of the world. Maree had kissed him back. He'd wanted to keep his distance until after he told her the truth, but he couldn't regret their kiss.

He turned back to check that she was still there. She was watching him with a dazed look on her face, her summer dress fluttering in the breeze around her legs. She looked so beautiful she took his breath away. He smiled and her face lit up.

He heard the roar of a motor coming closer and looked up. A black car was speeding down the street. Suddenly it veered and headed for Maree. Tom shouted her name as he started to run. Her eyes widened and her face was shocked. She started to turn away, but the car was too close.

His whole body surged toward her as the car loomed larger, the tires squealing as it rode up the sidewalk. Tom leaped forward and scooped Maree in his arms, pushing her out of the way. He twisted in the air so that she was on top and as he hit the sidewalk with his right hip, his head banged onto the concrete.

Maree fell out of his arms and rolled a few times. He reached for her, but it was hard to move. Everything felt far away and his head was spinning. He turned to look down the street as the car sped off with a screech of tires. He tried to catch the license plate, but the back bumper was mud splattered.

He blacked out for a few seconds. When he came to, Maree was looking down at him, her face creased with concern.

'Tom, wake up,' she called, gently stroking his cheek.

He heard the thud of footprints as people ran out of the restaurant.

'Please call an ambulance,' Maree shouted, lifting Tom's head onto her lap.

'Are you all right?' he asked.

'Yes,' Maree smiled. 'What about you?'

He tried to focus on her face, but suddenly he was seeing two of her. He felt something sticky cover his eye. Maree brushed his forehead with her skirt and he saw it was red with blood. He had something important he had to tell her, but he couldn't think what. Suddenly he remembered.

'I'm sorry.' He was so tired. 'It's all my fault.'

He'd known that if the stalker found out about Maree, she might want to hurt her. He should have stayed away until the private investigator had more information.

His eyes fluttered closed again.

'Wake up, Tom!' Maree called.

He jerked awake, letting out a groan.

'You might have concussion. You can't fall asleep.'

He knew she was right, but it was getting hard to fight the need to close his eyes.

The ambulance arrived and the paramedics briskly performed their examinations. They lifted Tom onto a stretcher and into the ambulance. Maree sat beside him, holding his hand. The paramedic wound a bandage around his head to stem the bleeding. He looked down and saw his shirt was torn and there was a nasty graze on his torso.

His eyes fluttered closed and Maree called him. He opened his eyes and saw her watching him with concern. He recognized the look in her eye. It was the same look she gave Beau. He felt warmth in his chest; she had feelings for him.

They arrived at the hospital and Tom was wheeled away, while a nurse waylaid Maree for details.

'Is there someone we should call?' he heard the nurse ask before he moved out of earshot. The orderly wheeled him into an examination room where a doctor checked his reflexes and other vital signs, and then they took him in for tests. It was an hour before he was transferred to a hospital room.

'Where's Maree, the woman I came with?' he asked the nurse as she checked his chart.

'She's in the waiting room. I'll go get her.'

Tom was watching the doorway when Maree rushed in, tears on her face. She came to his side and stroked his head.

Carter followed and stood against the wall. 'Are you all right?' he asked Tom.

'My head's pounding, but no lasting damage.' Tom turned back to Maree. 'What about you?'

'I'm fine. Just some scrapes and bruises.' She gestured to the dried blood on her bare knee.

'You're bleeding. You have to get that treated.'

'I'll get it checked in a minute.' She bit her lip to stem her tears. 'I can't believe you did that for me. That you saved me like that.'

'Of course,' Tom said. 'I would do anything for you.'

He'd felt such bone-chilling fear when he saw the car coming toward her. He knew now that he wanted nothing to come between them, especially not his lies. He had to trust that the feelings they had for each other would overcome her hurt and betrayal.

'Maree, there's something I have to tell—'

Carter cleared his throat. Tom had forgotten that he was still there.

'I hate to interrupt the lovebirds,' Carter said. 'But Tom and I need to talk.'

'It can wait.' Tom waved him away. He didn't want Maree to leave. He had to tell her now.

'No, it can't.' Carter came around and took Maree's hand and led her out of the room. 'Why don't you get your wound tended to by the nurse while we talk.'

'Dammit, Carter,' Tom sat up in the bed. 'Get her back here. I need to tell her the truth about Beau.'

'That's the last thing you need to do.' Carter eased him gently back down. 'You do that and she'll run in the other direction, which is something we can't afford right now.'

'What are you talking about?' Tom demanded.

'You realize who did this?' Carter asked.

Tom nodded. 'It was the stalker. I should have stayed away from Maree until we found out who it was.'

He leaned back against the pillow feeling defeated. Ever since he met Maree he'd brought her nothing but pain, when all he wanted to do was give her happiness.

'It wouldn't have made any difference.' Carter pulled out a note from his pocket and handed it to Tom.

Tom recognized the paper and formatting. It was another letter from the stalker. As he read, his vision darkened. 'Goddamn it, she knows about Beau.'

The stalker had been following him while he was undercover as Beau and knew all about his relationship with Maree. He felt a chill along his skin as he realized the stalker knew a lot more about him than he'd thought.

'That's right,' Carter said. 'You need to keep Maree safe and the only way to do that is if she doesn't know your big secret.'

Tom tamped down his anger and thought about it. He'd promised himself that he wouldn't touch Maree until he told her the truth. He'd wanted everything they did together to be real with no more secrets and lies. He tried to resist kissing her, but he'd realized it was his only chance to hold her in the near future. Once she knew the truth she would be angry and would need time to process it.

He'd poured all his love into that kiss and he knew she'd felt it. When he'd looked into her eyes afterwards he saw something he hadn't seen before. She had feelings for him, even though she might not be ready to admit it to herself. Beau had devastated her and made her doubt her instincts. Tom knew this was the moment to tell her the truth, before she fell too deep and while she could still forgive him. If he let things go any further between them her sense of betrayal would be too great.

'I can still tell her,' Tom said. 'She needs to know the truth. The longer I lie to her, the worse it's going to be when she finds out.'

'What do you think will happen when she finds out?' Carter asked.

'She'll be angry,' Tom said.

'Angry enough that she won't want to see you for a while?'

Tom nodded.

'Angry enough that if you told her that the two of you needed to go to a hideout together because of the stalker, she might think it was another trick?'

Tom sighed, feeling beaten.

'I've got a plan,' Carter said. 'The two of you go to my cabin. I'll have my security detail assigned to you. We'll draw your stalker out and then have her arrested.'

'And how am I supposed to convince Maree to come with me to the cabin?' Tom asked, feeling his head begin to ache again.

'Leave that to me.' Carter patted his shoulder. 'You just tell her about the stalker.' He left the room to get Maree.

While Carter was gone Tom tried to think through what was the best thing to do. He agreed with Carter to a point, but he knew that this decision wasn't just about now. It was about the forever Tom wanted them to have. By making this choice he was jeopardizing their future.

Carter returned with Maree. She had a white bandage strapped to her knee. Tom nodded and Carter left, closing the door behind him.

'Are you all right?' Tom reached for her.

'All good.' Maree sat on his bed and took his hand in hers. 'What about you? Your poor head.' She gently touched his bandage.

'It's okay.' Tom winced as the hammering started up in his head again.

'I should leave you to rest.' Maree went to get up.

'Not yet.' Tom held her back. 'There's something I need to tell you.'

'It can wait,' Maree patted his hand.

'No it can't,' he insisted. 'I owe you the truth.'

He hadn't realized until this moment that he was going to tell her everything, but it felt right. He couldn't lie anymore.

Maree's phone rang.

'I'm sorry about this.' She rifled through her purse and found her phone, pressing the button to turn it off. 'That's strange. I have five missed calls from my neighbor. And she's sent me a text message.' Maree frowned as she looked at the screen. 'Oh God,' she gasped. 'My house is on fire.'

'What?' Tom said, hoping he'd heard wrong.

'The firefighters are there.' Her eyes were wide with shock. 'I need to make a phone call.'

She walked away to the window and dialed. Tom listened to her one-sided conversation.

'No, no, that can't be right,' Maree said into the phone. 'I haven't turned on the stove for weeks now.'

After she hung up she looked into the distance for a moment.

'What happened?'

'The firefighters think the fire might have started from my gas stove, but I don't understand ...'

His skin broke out in goosepimples.

She walked to the bed and picked up her handbag. 'I've got to go,' she said, taking a step and almost stumbling.

He reached for her arm. 'You can't go by yourself.'

'I'll be fine.' Her voice wavered as she spoke.

'No,' Tom said. 'There's something you need to know. The car climbing the curb wasn't an accident.'

'What do you mean? Of course it was.'

'You know I have a stalker, and I think she's the one who was in the car.'

'A stalker,' Maree repeated.

'I think she might have had something to do with your house as well.'

Maree stared at him.

He saw the moment it hit her. Watching the light go out in her eyes and knowing he was the one responsible made him hate himself. He wanted to protect her from the world, yet he kept hurting her.

'I'm sorry. If I thought she would do something like this I never would have put you in danger,' Tom said.

Maree still looked dazed. 'It's okay.' She patted him on the arm. 'It's not your fault.'

Even now when she was in so much pain, she was comforting him. He felt like a heel.

'I have to go.' She gestured toward the door.

'Of course.' Tom reluctantly let go of her arm. 'Carter can take you.'

She nodded.

Tom called out to Carter. He poked his head in and Tom told him about Maree's house.

'Can you please take her?' Tom asked.

Carter nodded.

'I'll see you later,' Tom said to Maree's back, but she didn't turn around.

As he watched her leave the room he was full of foreboding. The stalker was escalating the violence. They weren't safe. He hadn't even told her the truth about himself, yet already he had caused her so much damage to her life. Was there any way for him to atone for all the ways he had hurt her?

Chapter 15

Maree walked out of the hospital room with Carter, still reeling from Tom's confession. His stalker had tried to kill her. She felt shaky from the knowledge that someone wanted to deliberately hurt her. She looked at the phone and felt tears well up in her eyes. Her house. Her beautiful home.

'I know it's a lot to take in,' Carter said, holding her arm. 'I've arranged for security.'

At any other time Maree would have been outraged at how far her life was spinning out of control, but after her conversation with Tom all she felt was paranoia. Someone had been watching her without her knowing. They knew where she lived, where she worked, and she had been completely unaware of the danger she was in. She looked around warily. Someone could be watching her right now and she wouldn't know. She caught the eye of the nurse behind the nurse's station. The nurse met her eyes with concern. She could be the stalker and Maree would never know.

'Maree, Maree?' Carter repeated.

She realized he'd said her name more than once. She blinked and looked back at him.

'There's no need to be worried,' Carter said soothingly. 'We're just covering all bases. This is Ross.' He introduced her to a tall, blond, buff man in the corridor. 'Ross will take us to your house. And I've arranged for Tony to stand on guard outside Tom's hospital room.' Carter pointed to another buff man in black.

Carter led her to the elevator. Maree stepped in and Ross stood next to her. His looming shadow would usually make her feel slightly intimidated, but today she was glad to have someone of his size around.

When they got to the lobby, Carter sent Ross to get the car and bring it to the front entrance while the two of them sat in the waiting room. The media had caught wind of Tom's accident and were camped out the front of the hospital. Ross returned with the car and Carter helped Maree stand. The day was catching up with her. The bruises she'd collected while landing on the sidewalk were aching.

Carter held her arm as they walked out. Light bulbs started flashing.

'That's her,' a voice shouted. 'That's his latest squeeze.'

Maree saw the mob of journalists gathered outside the hospital gates.

'Hey, over here,' someone called out, wanting to get a facial shot. 'How did it feel when the car was headed for you?'

'Who do you think was behind the attack?' another yelled.

'How long have you and Calvert been an item?' a third called.

Maree was inured to their tricks. She'd had plenty of practice evading the paparazzi while she was with her father. She determinedly kept looking down at the ground, letting her hair obscure her face and frustrate the photographers. Carter put his arm around her shoulders and hugged her close to him, blocking her from view as they walked briskly to the car. He opened the back door and Maree climbed in. As soon as she was cocooned in the silence of the car, the journalists' shouts were drowned out.

Maree kept her head down and let her hair do the work. She wasn't going to crouch down beside the seat and act like she had something to hide or she was ashamed, but she also wasn't going to help some photographer get his trophy shot either.

'Turn left here.' Maree gave Ross directions.

'I have your address,' Ross said. 'We're not going straight there. First we have to make sure we haven't got a tail.'

Maree looked behind and sure enough, there were a few cars tailing them. She sank deeper into the back seat.

While Carter explained to Ross about her house being on fire, Maree began to shake. This was the first time she'd had a quiet moment since she got to the hospital. She'd spent the whole time pacing, her body full of nerves. The doctors had used terms like 'bleeding on the brain', and her blood had run cold. People died every day from head injuries, and she'd been deathly afraid that would happen to Tom.

She remembered when they first arrived at the hospital Tom had been wheeled away on a stretcher, while a nurse had asked if there was someone to call. Maree had remembered Carter's name from their lunch date and the nurse found his number in Tom's cell phone.

When Carter had rushed into the waiting room, she'd explained what happened. She'd flashbacked to that moment on the street, watching Tom walk away after their kiss. As she'd seen his expression change to fear, she'd been full of confusion until she saw the car. She'd turned back to see Tom throw himself in front of the car with no regard for his own safety, the way he'd curved his body around hers and taken the brunt of their fall, protecting her from the bruising concrete.

'It was aiming for you?' Carter had asked when she finished telling him the events leading up to the accident.

'Yes, well, I don't know. They might have lost control and climbed the sidewalk.'

'But did they stop?' Carter asked.

Maree had to concentrate. She'd been so panicked when it all happened that her head was spinning. She remembered shouting at the bystanders to ring for an ambulance. She'd seen the car from the corner of her eye. It had been standing in the middle of the street and then it accelerated away.

'The car stopped, but they didn't get out and then they sped off.'

Maree felt sick as she relived the horror. What sort of a person nearly hits someone and speeds off? She'd assumed it was a drunk driver too scared of the penalty if they got caught.

There had been something in Carter's face that gave her pause, but just then the doctor had walked in.

'Tom will be fine,' the doctor had said. 'He's just got a slight concussion and we'll be keeping him overnight.'

Maree had felt her knees give out as she held onto a chair and lowered herself to sit. She felt such overwhelming relief. Tom was going to be all right.

In that moment she had realized her feelings for Tom were strong. He'd gotten under her skin and she wanted the opportunity to explore what they had together. She'd been quick to dismiss him as a playboy actor whose goal was to charm as many women as he could, but there was depth to Tom. The two of them could talk about so many things and they really clicked together. When she remembered their kiss and the feeling of deja vu that had tantalized her, her stomach fluttered with excitement.

She came back to the present. Ross hit the accelerator and the car sped through a red light, pushing her against the back seat.

'Sorry about that,' Ross said, as their eyes met in the mirror. 'But at least I got rid of them.'

Maree peered through the back window and saw that no one was following them anymore. She sighed with relief.

She looked around to get her bearings. They would be home in ten minutes. She'd spent the drive thinking about Tom and the accident so she could avoid thinking about what was waiting for her. But now she felt a chill across her skin. What was she going to find when they got home?

Ross turned into her street and Maree peered across the front seat. The street was crowded. There were fire engines and police cars in front of her house, and bystanders crowded on the sidewalk opposite.

'We'll have to get out here. 'I'll go with Maree while you stay with the car,' he told Ross.

Carter opened the car door for her. Maree was still looking out the windshield. Carter offered her his arm and she got out, her legs feeling shaky. They walked up the sidewalk toward the house.

A police officer stopped them.

'This is Maree Reynard, she's the owner of the house,' Carter explained.

After Maree showed him her driver's license the police officer lifted the tape and they ducked under. At first the trees and shrubs protected her from the reality. It was only as they walked further up the driveway that Maree saw the black gaping hole where her living room used to be. She felt like she'd been punched in the gut.

A firefighter approached and introduced himself as the Fire Marshal. 'Someone broke down the front door and poured gasoline in the living room. The fire spread quickly, but we were able to salvage the bedrooms.'

Maree covered her mouth as she began to cry. Her house was her sanctuary, the one thing she had that was her own. Moving out to her mother's house she'd found a home for the first time. Pain welled inside her as she looked at her beautiful furniture, her belongings, now destroyed.

Carter squeezed her shoulders and held her tighter against him. 'Is she able to go inside and get some of her things?'

'I'll get someone to take you through. We've assessed the building structure in the back rooms and it's stable,' the Fire Marshall said.

They followed another firefighter down the hallway to her bedroom. It was untouched by fire, but the smell of smoke permeated everything.

'You'll have to get your clothes dry-cleaned before you can wear them,' Carter said while Maree stood at the threshold.

He led her into the bedroom and rifled through her closet. He handed her a suitcase. She turned toward him, her whole body shutting down. She found it hard to concentrate.

'You start packing while I speak to the police,' said Carter.

Maree nodded. She walked over to her closet and reached out a hand, feeling the softness of her clothes. The acrid smell of smoke burned her nostrils. Her legs gave out and she collapsed into the closet. She buried her face into her thick coat, muffling the sound of her crying.

It shouldn't matter so much—after all, they were just things. But it did matter. Someone was deliberately targeting her. Wanting to hurt her. Wanting to hurt Tom. Oh, God—Tom. As she thought of him, defenseless and alone in the hospital, her own grief lifted. She didn't have time for this. She needed to make sure he was all right. She stood up and wiped her face, before quickly throwing some things into the bag.

Carter returned. 'I'm so sorry,' he said, as he picked up her suitcase. 'Tom will pay for everything to be repaired.'

'It's fine. Is Tom all right?' she asked.

'I just checked on him and Tony's on the job. He's got a list of hospital staff on roster and he's making sure no one else gets past him. Have you got a friend you can stay with? Or I can put you up in a hotel if you prefer.'

'That won't be necessary,' Maree said. 'I want to go back to the hospital.'

Carter's eyes widened. 'There's no need. Tom's resting for the night. He's all right, I told you.'

'I'm sure he is, but I want us to spend the night together. I'd feel much better knowing that all of us were there to make sure no one hurts him tonight.' Maree took a deep breath and walked out of the bedroom and down the hallway. She kept her eyes straight ahead, not looking at what used to be her living room.

'Tom said you were special.' Carter stepped in beside her outside of the house.

'He told you about me?'

'Yes, he did.'

Maree was about to ask him how Tom felt about her, but she stilled the words on her tongue. She didn't have to ask. She already knew. She knew from the way he kissed her and she knew from the way he had protected her. The only question was, how did she feel about him? As she pondered that she realized there were too many emotions in the way. All she knew was that right now she wanted to be with him. She couldn't think any further than that.

'I told the investigators about the hit and run and that it was probably connected to the fire,' Carter was saying.

There was something in his tone that put Maree on edge. 'But they didn't believe you?' she asked.

Carter sighed with frustration. 'They want to take a statement from you and Tom tomorrow morning and then they will investigate further.' They'd reached the car and he opened the door for her.

After Carter placed her suitcase in the trunk he came and sat in the back with her. 'I'm worried about Tom. I want him to leave town and recover somewhere he can be safe. I have a cabin at Lake Arrowhead and he can go there, but he won't leave without you.'

'I can't leave town,' Maree said. 'What about my job?'

'I can speak to the director. You're still in pre-production, and you can design from anywhere. I have a home office I can set up with everything you'll need. And most importantly the two of you will be safe until the police find the stalker.'

'But the two of us ... We're not—'

'Don't worry, the cabin has three bedrooms. It's very spacious and you can each have a room,' Carter broke in as if he was reading her thoughts.

Maree hesitated for a moment. She didn't feel right about leaving town. She felt like the stalker was winning by chasing her away, but she had to think about Tom. He was badly hurt and needed a chance to recover, and she needed some time to be able to process everything that happened.

A thought stirred. 'But what if the stalker follows us?' Maree asked.

'We've got it covered. Tony and Ross will be driving in separate cars behind you to make sure that no one is following. And if someone is, they'll take care of them. They're going to stay at a friend's cabin next door and keep an eye on you both.' Carter smiled reassuringly. 'We now know what the stalker is capable of and we won't be underestimating her again.'

'But first we need to go to my friend Allegra's house. I need to borrow some clothes,' Maree said.

Carter nodded and she gave Ross directions. She called Allegra on her cell phone and told her about the fire. After her initial shock at the news, Allegra told her where to find the spare key and said she would meet her there.

When they arrived at Allegra's house, Ross and Carter remained by the car while Maree let herself in. She'd started going through Allegra's closet, trying to compile a list in her head of must-haves, when she heard the front door open and Allegra call her name.

'In the bedroom,' Maree replied.

She heard the click of Allegra's heels as she walked down the hardwood hallway. 'How are you doing?' Allegra asked when she reached the bedroom and bundled Maree into an embrace.

Maree teared up, but she was spent. 'I think I'm numb.' She stepped away and winced. She sat on the bed and stretched out her leg. The wound on her knee was throbbing.

'What happened?' Allegra asked as she saw the bandage.

Maree hadn't told her about the hit and run on the phone. Allegra's eyes widened with shock as Maree caught her up on her day.

'I don't know what to say.' Allegra sat shakily on the bench seat in front of her vanity mirror. 'First what's his name turns out to be a fraud, and now your rebound guy is responsible for destroying your life one piece at a time. The way you're going you could be dead in a week.'

Maree opened her mouth for a rebuttal, but soon realized she had nothing. Her eyes caught Allegra's. They had a conversation like this at least once a month, except usually it was Maree being the voice of reason as she commented on Allegra's train-wreck of a love life. A smile broke out on Maree's face and she quickly looked away.

'It's not funny,' Allegra said.

Maree started giggling uncontrollably. It wasn't funny, and yet it was. Allegra picked up a powder puff and threw it at Maree. Maree caught it and fell back on the bed as she laughed. Allegra joined her and soon they were rolling around until their stomachs ached.

When the hysteria stopped Maree stared at the ceiling.

Allegra leaned on her elbow and looked at her. 'What are you going to do?'

Maree shrugged. 'Carter wants me and Tom to go to his cabin.'

'No way. You stay here. You need to put distance between the two of you. This guy is dangerous.'

Maree sat up. 'I'm going with him.'

She hadn't realized until that moment that she wanted to be with Tom. The option had been presented to her as something she couldn't refuse, but she had choices. She could stay with Allegra or in a hotel. She could get away from Tom until the stalker issue was resolved, but she didn't want to.

'Why?' Allegra tugged her arm. 'Do you feel like you owe him because he could have died saving you? Fact is, you wouldn't have been in danger in the first place if it wasn't for him.'

'No. It's because I want to be with him. I want the chance to explore what's between us.'

'Oh, no.' Allegra covered her face with her hands. 'You've fallen for him.' She stood and began to pace. 'I should have known that you couldn't just enjoy some no-strings sex, that feelings would get involved.' Her face scrunched up as if she were talking about faeces.

'I need to get going.' Maree gestured toward the closet where Allegra's vintage treasures hung. 'Can you find me some regular clothes?'

Allegra tsked as she opened drawers and prepared stacks of clothing. 'Are you sure you want to do this?'

Maree nodded, smiling. 'I'm a big girl, Mom. I'll be fine.'

'No, you won't.' Allegra found a travel bag and packed the clothes into it. 'But if anything goes wrong you call me.'

Maree held out her hands and Allegra helped her off the bed. 'Will do.'

Allegra walked her out, carrying the bag. Carter came to the door and Allegra handed the bag to him. 'Make sure nothing happens to her.'

Carter smiled and took hold of the handle. 'Of course.'

Allegra held tight, forcing him closer. 'I will make you a eunuch if anything happens to her.'

Carter's eyes widened and he looked to Maree. She shrugged. Allegra was wearing her mobster girlfriend face. She was capable of anything in a temper.

'I promise she'll be safe,' Carter assured her. 'I have an investigator looking for the stalker, and there will be bodyguards at the cabin taking care of Maree and Tom.'

Allegra nodded and released the bag.

As the car drove off Maree waved through the back windshield. Allegra stood on the sidewalk, her face wreathed in concern. Maree knew she should feel concerned too. She was possibly in danger—there was a stalker who was after her and meant to harm her—but she felt strangely calm. It was like there was an upper limit for how much fear you could feel and she'd reached it. She just wanted to see Tom and make sure he was okay, and then she wanted to sleep.

They went to Tom's house, and after Carter had packed him a suitcase they returned to the hospital. Tom was sleeping. He fought to open his eyes, and when he saw Maree he tried to sit up. 'How's your house?' he asked.

'It's okay. Just a few household items were damaged. Nothing that can't be repaired.' Even though she tried to sound casual, her voice caught in her throat.

'Tell me the truth,' said Tom.

Maree told him about the living room.

'I am so sorry.' He took her hand.

'Don't apologize. All that matters is that no one was hurt,' she said bravely. 'Now, I'm going to brush my teeth and ask the nurse for a cot.'

She left the room before her emotions overcame her. By the time she came back Carter was gone and Ross had taken over the shift from Tony. Maree had changed into her pajamas and the cot was set up beside Tom's bed. She lay down, her body aching. She'd washed up in the hospital bathroom but she felt like there was grime still sticking to her body.

'I'm sorry you've been dragged into all this,' Tom whispered into the darkness. He'd turned on his side and was looking at her.

'It's not your fault.' She turned on her side too, so they were facing each other.

'It is. I knew about the stalker. I knew she was dangerous. I should have stayed away.'

Maree felt let down. If he had stayed away, she wouldn't have seen him. 'Did you want to stay away?' she asked, keeping still in the darkness as she waited for his reply.

'I couldn't keep away from you.'

She felt a warmth inside.

'I promise I won't let anything happen to you,' he said.

Maree yawned, the tiredness of the day catching up with her.

'Go to sleep.' Tom reached down and took her hand, squeezing it gently.

She could feel his eyes on her face, but the pull of sleep was too great.

Maree woke with a gasp when something banged. Bright light was flooding the room and Tom's bed was empty. Then he walked in from the bathroom, wearing jeans and a T-shirt. He smiled when he saw that she was awake.

'Hello sleepyhead,' he said, as he perched on the bed.

She sat up in the cot. 'How are you feeling?'

'Still banged up,' Tom sighed. The bandage was off his head and there were grazes on his cheek. 'But a few days' rest will make it all better.'

Maree got out of the cot and started folding her bedding.

'Carter's on his way here,' Tom said. 'He'll take us to the police station to make a statement. He thought it might be safer if he drove us to the cabin.'

'I'll be ready in ten minutes.' She got a change of clothes from her suitcase and went to the bathroom.

·♥·♥·♥·♥·♥·

After they finished at the police station, Maree insisted on sitting at the front so that Tom could relax in the back. The police interview had taken a lot out of him and he had to take his pain pills. They barely spoke. Tom mostly had his head back and was sleeping.

An hour later they arrived at the cabin. As Carter parked, Maree leaned forward to look out the window. The log cabin was on a slope, nestled among pine trees, their scent bringing to mind Christmas. As they walked up the porch stairs she turned and surveyed the view. They were halfway up a hill, and Lake Arrowhead stretched before her with white-capped mountains behind it.

Carter unlocked the front door and showed them through. 'Home sweet home,' he said. 'Well, I should say it's my home away from home.'

'How come I never knew about this?' Tom asked as he looked around the rustic cabin.

'This belonged to my mother's family and it's been passed down. I used to come here all the time when I was a child, but now not so much.' A shadow of regret crossed Carter's face 'Anyway, I'll give you the grand tour.'

The cabin had high cathedral ceilings and a stone fireplace in each room. The light-colored wood reflected the sunlight and it felt light and airy. The designer in Maree admired the décor—from the faux antler chandelier to the sage throw casually placed on the sofa, just inviting one to sit down and snuggle under it.

Maree carried her suitcase to one of the bedrooms, her hands reaching out to caress the patchwork quilt coverlet on the bed. She couldn't wait to sink into its softness.

'A friend has stocked the pantry and Ross and Tony will handle future orders as part of their security detail,' Carter said as he walked toward the front door. 'The two of you need to stay here and do nothing.'

After Carter left, Maree stood gazing out the floor-to-ceiling window at the view of the lake. She turned toward Tom and saw that he looked pale, his mouth bracketed by lines of pain.

'You need to lie down.' She came to his side and led him to the bedroom.

She sat him on the bed and helped him take off his boots. He was squinting from the bright light flooding the room. 'Where are your pajamas?' she asked as she closed the curtains.

He pointed to his bag.

'Do you need me to bring your medication?'

He nodded. 'Thanks.'

After she got him his pajamas, Maree left the room and closed the door behind her. She filled a glass of water and found his pain pills.

When she returned to the bedroom she gently knocked on the door. Tom called out to enter, and she opened it. He was lying in bed, his brow still furrowed from pain. He took the glass from her and swallowed the tablets. 'Thank you,' he whispered as he lay back again.

'You rest.' She caressed his forehead, feeling his soft hair under her hand.

He took her hand and held it to his lips, kissing her wrist. 'I'm glad you're here,' he murmured.

'Me too.'

Seeing he was drifting to sleep, Maree tiptoed out and closed the door.

Now that that she had the cabin to herself there was only one thing she wanted to do. She returned the glass to the kitchen and hot-footed it to the bathroom. As she turned the tap and listened to the sound of flowing water filling the tub, she felt herself relaxing. She sank into the bath and sighed with relief. The hot water surrounded her, and she felt her aches and pains ease. As she thought about the possibilities of the next few days she felt butterflies flutter in her stomach. She scooped the bubble foam from the surface and blew into her hand, sending the bubbles floating on the air. She was excited about being with Tom. The cabin was so romantic, and anything could happen. She laid her head against the bath and smiled.

<h1 style="text-align:center">Chapter 16</h1>

Tom woke, and for a moment he didn't know where he was. As sleep cleared he recognized the wood-panelled ceiling above him and remembered he was at Carter's cabin. He could hear sounds in the kitchen and a delicious smell teased his nostrils. He dressed in jeans and a T-shirt, and went to find Maree in the kitchen, grilling steaks on the stove.

'How long have I been asleep?' Tom asked.

'On and off for two days.'

'Really?'

'But it looks like all that sleeping did you good,' she said with a smile.

Tom smiled back as he sat on a stool. He felt much better. His headache had faded and he was feeling a little less achy.

'I've made a salad and some baked potatoes.' Maree pointed to the oven.

Tom's stomach rumbled. 'Now I know I'm feeling better,' he said. 'Because I'm ravenous.'

He enjoyed watching her as she cooked. There was a faint sheen of perspiration on her face and hair was escaping from her ponytail, tendrils fluttering around her face. She was dressing the salad when a lock of hair dropped in front of her face. She blew, trying to push it away.

'Let me.' Tom got up and collected the strand, moving it to the back of her head and twisting it in a loop around her ponytail.

She paused with her hands in the salad bowl. 'Thank you.'

He stood in front of her, his hand at the back of her head. It would be the most natural thing in the world to draw her toward him and kiss her. Her eyes darkened with desire and her lips parted as she waited. He leaned down and their lips touched. He brushed her lips, once, twice and pressed into her. She opened her mouth to him and he held her tighter. He wanted nothing more than to sink into this moment, sink into her, and feel her against him. He went to move the salad bowl out of the way, when reality returned and he realized what he was doing.

He pulled back. Maree was breathless, and he was panting.

'I'll set the table,' he said and quickly turned away.

As he took cutlery from the drawer he fought for breath. That was close. For a moment he had forgotten everything, including the fact that he was lying to her. This should have been a dream come true—a romantic getaway with the woman he loved—instead it was his biggest nightmare. He had to make sure their relationship remained strictly platonic. He couldn't trick her again by making love to her under false pretenses, not to mention the fact that if they made love she might realize that Beau and Tom were one and the same.

Tom laid the cutlery and returned to the kitchen. Maree was serving. He took their plates and carried them to the table. They sat across from each other.

'This smells delicious,' he said.

'It tastes even better.' Maree lifted the fork to her mouth.

His mouth watered as she saw her red lips and he quickly looked down at his plate.

Tom took a bite. 'You're right,' he said. 'It does taste even better.'

Maree smiled and sipped from her wineglass.

Everything about the moment was working against him. The lamps produced a romantic glow, bathing everything in luminescence, and together with good food and wine, this was a perfect romantic dinner. Under any other circumstances it would be obvious where this was leading. Tom glanced at the bedroom door and quickly tore his eyes away. That couldn't happen.

'I was thinking we could watch a movie after dinner,' Tom said.

Maree nodded.

When they finished they went to the living room Maree sat on the two-seater couch. Tom glanced at the armchair, but couldn't do that to her and so sat beside her, trying to create as much space as he could between them. The fire Carter had lit before he left was burning brightly, and with the dark windows outside, it felt like they were cocooned in a world of their own.

Maree hit play on the DVD player and *The Notebook* started playing. He hadn't realized when he let her pick a movie how fraught a choice it would be. He couldn't watch this with her. This was the movie you watched when you wanted to close the deal. What he needed was something to ruin the mood.

'God, I hate this guy,' Tom said. 'He dissed me at the Oscars a few years ago. Apparently my movie was too commercial for him.'

'Really?' Maree said. 'But he's such a gentleman. My friend was his makeup artist on *Drive* and she said he was lovely.'

'Well, your friend was a woman and he probably wanted to sleep with her,' Tom said, feeling guilty about lying. The truth was he'd met Ryan Gosling and he was a great guy, but that wasn't going to help him now. 'Do you mind if we pick something else?'

'Of course not.'

She handed him the remote and he ejected the movie. He went to the DVD cabinet and felt relief when he saw Carter's collection wouldn't let him down.

'This is really good.'

'What is it?' Maree asked.

'I'll let it be a surprise.' He put the DVD in, keeping the title of *Saw* out of her eyesight.

In the first scene there was a corpse on the floor and two men chained in a basement. He looked over at Maree and could tell by her stiff posture that she wasn't a fan of the horror genre. As the movie progressed he kept commentating on the body parts piling up and cheering as blood spurted out.

'I'm going to bed,' Maree said as soon as the movie finished. 'If I can get any sleep tonight,' she muttered under her breath.

'Good night.' Tom smiled as he watched her go. He'd made it through the first two days without giving into his romantic inclinations, now he had to keep it up. As he lay in bed he was aware that Maree was in the room next door. He felt like he could hear her breathing through the wall. He tossed and turned all night knowing that if he walked into her bedroom, she would welcome him.

The next morning Tom woke up early and started breakfast. He was scrambling eggs in a pan when Maree entered the kitchen. 'I thought I'd do breakfast since you made dinner last night.'

'Are you sure you're up for it?' she asked.

Tom smiled. 'I'm feeling much better.'

'Thanks.' Maree helped herself to coffee and sat at the table, sipping from the mug as she looked out the window. 'It's beautiful out there. Maybe we should go for a walk.'

As Tom served her eggs and bacon he weighed up the pros and cons. Walking through the woods sounded like a safe proposition. He looked out the window and decided otherwise. It was the sort of landscape that was just made for stolen kisses against tree trunks.

'I'm still feeling a bit weak,' Tom said. 'I think I'll rest in bed.'

Maree nodded, her face showing disappointment. 'I've got work to do too. It'd be better to get started after breakfast.'

They ate in silence. Maree stood when she finished. 'My turn to clean up.' She reached to take his plate, but he took hold of it.

'It's okay, I'll do it.'

'No, you're tired.' Maree took his plate and shooed him to the bedroom. 'Go to bed.'

Tom closed his bedroom door, feeling guilty about the confusion on her face. This was obviously not how she expected their stay to go, but he had no choice. He had to keep her at arm's length until the stalker was discovered and Maree was safe. Then he could tell her the truth. He sat on the bed and pulled his phone out of his pocket.

He messaged Carter. 'Any news?'

Tom waited five minutes. He was about to call Carter when he finally received a return message. 'Investigator is chasing a lead. He'll know something by tomorrow.'

Tom felt his legs go weak with relief. Thank God. He only had to get through today and one more night and it would be over. He could hear the sound of typing and peered into the study. Maree was at her computer. He lay on the bed and tried to nap, but he couldn't settle. He was feeling restless and hot. He checked his watch. An hour had passed. He got up and left the room again. The study door was closed now. He decided to go for a walk while Maree was distracted.

*

Maree sat in Carter's study and flipped through her sketchpad. A few days ago, developing her designs had been all she thought about, but now it seemed so far away. She sighed and put the sketchpad away and opened her laptop to answer emails. As she worked she felt sweat slip down her back. It was getting humid and she was finding it hard to concentrate. As she clicked through her inbox she was aware of the quiet in the cabin behind her while Tom was sleeping. While she knew that he needed time to recover, she couldn't help but be disappointed with the way things were progressing.

She had hoped that this getaway would give them an opportunity to further their relationship. *Stop being coy, Maree,* Allegra's voice whispered in her head. *You were hoping to get laid.* Maree blushed and covered her face with her hands. Even though Tom was nowhere around, she was embarrassed by how much she longed for him. Lying in bed the night before she had barely slept. Each creak of the cabin had made her flush with hope that Tom was walking from his room to hers. That he would just take her, and that she would feel his body against hers ... But he didn't come, and so she tossed and turned until she finally fell asleep somewhere around dawn. She should have been exhausted and in desperate need of a nap, but instead she felt unsettled. Her legs and back were feeling achy, probably from sitting too long.

She looked out the window and saw the trees swaying in the breeze. She was suddenly desperate to feel the wind cooling her skin. A walk was just what she needed. She slowly tiptoed out of the cabin, carrying her sandals. The day was beautiful, without a cloud in the sky. She hadn't walked far when she came to the lake. Suddenly the heat felt almost unbearable and her skin was on fire. She glanced back at the path leading to the cabin and thought about returning for her swimsuit. She looked around carefully. There wasn't a soul in sight. She couldn't wait, she desperately needed to cool down.

She was wearing matching lingerie, if anyone looked from a distance they would think she was wearing a bikini. She took off her shirt and shorts and hid them behind a rock so they weren't visible to passersby. She'd taken off her bandage that morning in the shower and a graze still remained. As she walked into the water her knee tingled, but soon the coolness soothed the red skin. She sighed with relief. This was just what she needed. She was floating on her back, the current gently rocking her to and fro as she stared up at the faint wisps of clouds against the blue sky, when she thought she heard something. She let her feet drift to the sandy bottom and listened. Someone was coming. She quickly ducked behind a large rock and sat in the water.

There was the sound of footsteps and then the hiker stopped. Maree hoped they would pass by. She just had to wait it out.

When the silence stretched out too long she peeped from behind the rock. Tom was on the beach. He was undoing his shorts and pulling them down his legs. Her mouth went dry. She knew that the right thing to do was to call out and let him know that she was in the water, but she couldn't make a sound to save her life. He took off his T-shirt and tossed it on the ground, revealing his taut chest and a nasty graze from the accident. Maree was torn between wanting to nurse him and the urge to glide over to him and run her tongue over his skin.

Her cheeks flushed. What was happening to her? She'd never lusted after a man like this. He was every woman's fantasy. Just looking at him made her wet. Tom walked into the water and Maree moved back to the rock.

'Hi,' she said, finally finding her tongue.

He turned to look at her and his face showed surprise. As his eyes dipped below the water and registered what she was wearing, she was gratified to see desire on his face, before he tore his eyes away.

'I was feeling hot,' Maree blurted out the first thing that came to mind.

'Me too,' Tom said.

An awkward silence descended. 'This is really nice.' Maree splashed water on her shoulders.

'Yes, it's nice.' Tom glanced at her, his eyes lingering on her beaded nipples.

Her whole body went into meltdown and her awkwardness faded. 'This looks like a good spot to enjoy the view.' She lifted herself on the rock.

There was a part of her that knew it was out of character to be so forward, but she was impatient to move their relationship to another level. Her skin was almost itchy with the need to feel him against her.

'Come sit with me.'

As he leaped out of the water and sat next to her, his wet white briefs left nothing to the imagination. Her skin felt like it was burning up and she didn't know if it was from the sun, or her desire for Tom. As he looked out at the view her eyes feasted hungrily on him.

He turned toward her and his gaze settled on her lips. *Please, please, please,* she pleaded in her head. She felt like she had been waiting a whole lifetime for his kiss and she could barely restrain herself from throwing herself at him. Tom leaned in, and finally they were kissing. His lips felt cool on hers as she tasted his tongue. She wanted to get closer. Her hands went around his neck and she pulled him to her. This was bliss. Her head was spinning and she felt like she was floating. It wasn't until they landed in the water that she realized that they'd been falling. She came out of the water laughing. Tom smiled and as his eyes crinkled up, and Maree had a moment of deja vu, the way his hair was slicked back ... Just as quickly it was gone.

Chapter 17

Tom felt such love when he saw the joy in her eyes. He wanted nothing more than to make love to her. He knew if they kissed again he wouldn't be able to stop. He shouldn't have kissed her in the first place, but he wasn't able to help himself. He hadn't realized he was leaning forward until his lips brushed against hers. He'd thought one kiss couldn't hurt, but now he was deceiving her again. Panic filled him. He had to stop this now.

A terrible idea came to him. He knew there was one word that would bring fear to Maree's eyes and end this. He hesitated. He didn't know if he could do it to her. As her lips responded against his, desperation filled him.

'Snake,' he said.

Maree's face blanched with terror. He pointed behind her. She didn't even look. She kicked out toward the beach, her foot connecting with his groin. He fell forward, clutching himself as his knees gave way, falling into the lake. Water invaded his nose and mouth. He stood up shakily, clutching the rock for support as he coughed and spluttered. Maree was already on the beach.

'Tom, hurry,' she screamed, her voice full of terror.

He walked out, waves of nausea and pain flowing over him
with every step.

'What happened?' Maree demanded when he reached the
beach. 'Did the snake bite you?' She began examining his torso
and fell to her knees as she touched his legs.

'No, I fell.' He didn't want her to feel bad about hurting him.
After all it was his own fault. He knew what would happen when
he said snake. 'I think I need to lie down.'

Maree collected their clothes and he put his arm around her
shoulders for support. As they stumbled toward the cabin he
smiled weakly. It wasn't all bad. At least he didn't have to worry
about romance anymore. From the throbbing in his groin he
knew he wouldn't be experiencing an erection anytime soon.

Maree helped him into bed. She was still wearing only her
underwear and bra. As she leaned over and helped arrange his
pillow, her breast was in his face, the nipple almost on his lips.
All he needed to do was lift his head half an inch and it would
be in his mouth. When he felt no response in his body at the
thought he didn't know whether to feel relief or fear.

'Do you need help taking off your underwear?' Maree asked.

Tom met her eyes. She was looking at him with concern. She
was beautiful, wet tendrils of hair curling around her breasts,
the high-cut underwear showing off her smooth legs.

'I can do it,' he said.

Maree nodded and backed out of the room.

After she left he sat up in bed. His stomach rolled with nausea
as he slipped off his wet underwear. He lay back and covered
himself with a sheet. One more day down. He closed his eyes
and eventually fell asleep. He dreamed of Maree. They were
entwined in bed, his hands caressing her golden skin.

When he woke up there was a tent in the sheets. It was
the only time in his life he was unhappy to wake up with an
erection. He'd been hoping he would be out of commission until
tomorrow at least, when Carter would tell him who the stalker
was and Tom could tell Maree the truth.

Hearing music, he got dressed and went to the kitchen. Maree was dancing as she stirred a saucepan. She was wearing denim cut-offs that made her legs go on forever, and a white shirt with the ends tied at the front showing off her midriff. He felt desire punch him in the gut.

'Here, taste this.' She brought the wooden spoon to his lips before he had a chance to answer.

He automatically opened his mouth and the smooth chocolate sauce lit up his tastebuds. 'That's delicious.'

She smiled. 'Oh good. I suddenly had a craving for chocolate cake and we had all the ingredients.' She nodded to the chocolate cake resting on the sideboard.

Tom sat on the kitchen stool and watched her. He was mesmerized by a rivulet of sweat that ran down her neck and between her cleavage. As she stirred the sauce her breasts bounced and he bit his bottom lip to hold back a moan.

'Do you need help?' he asked, his voice husky with desire.

She smiled over her shoulder. 'Nearly done. I will, however, need your help eating it.'

He gulped. Now all he could imagine was the chocolate sauce glistening on her skin as he feasted on her body.

'Tony brought over a trout he caught so I've prepared it with rice and a salad.' Maree removed the saucepan from the hotplate and turned off the stove. She took two white plates from the rack and wiped them with a dish towel. She lifted the lid off the frypan and the delicious smell of fried fish filled the kitchen. Within a few moments she'd served dinner and handed him his plate. 'I thought we could sit on the porch and look at the view as we ate.' She picked up her glass of wine and walked ahead.

Tom followed, nearly tripping on the rug because he was too busy watching her backside. Maree sat on the porch seat with a sigh. The sun was setting and the water sparkled, the breeze teased tendrils of her hair around her face. As he ate Tom kept sneaking glances at her. She took his breath away.

She caught him and their eyes held. He kept telling himself to look away, but he couldn't. He saw her eyes darken with desire. The romance of the moment settled over him and he had to fight the inevitability that he felt. He kept remembering his dream, Maree lying beneath him, her face wreathed with desire.

After they finished dinner she got up and took his plate. 'I'll be back with dessert.'

He nodded, unable to say anything. She returned a moment later and handed him a plate with a slice of chocolate cake drizzled with sauce. He inhaled the aroma of the sauce and felt his mouth water. Maree sat back down. She took a bite, her eyes closed in ecstasy as she moaned. Tom felt his appetite shift. All he wanted was to inhale her mouth and taste the chocolate sauce on her tongue.

'Don't you like it?' Maree nodded toward his untouched cake.

The spell broken Tom was finally able to look away and eat. 'It's delicious.' He didn't look at her, too scared he would be mesmerized once again.

'That was heavenly.' Maree sighed when she finished. She placed her plate on the table between them and sat back.

Tom finished, forcing the rest of the cake down, and then he put his plate on top of hers. The sun had set and the breeze from the lake had a chill to it. 'Maybe we should go inside.'

'Why?' Maree stood and spread her arms wide. 'The breeze is beautiful.'

She was flushed, her eyes closed as she reveled in the zephyr. Even though Tom was burning with desire, he still felt the chill biting into his skin.

'Let's go.'

Maree seemed not to hear him. He took her hand and led her inside. As they entered the cabin she pushed him against the wall and leaned in closer. His heart beat faster at her proximity and the wildness in her eyes.

He evaded her kiss. 'I think we need to stop.'

'Why?' She was leaning against his chest, her arms around her waist.

'Because ...' His thoughts deserted him and all he wanted was to feel. He just wanted to wrap his arms around her and hold her tightly. He took a deep shuddering breath.

'I can't concentrate.' Their eyes caught and he didn't hide his desire.

'I don't want you to.' Maree licked her lips.

He put his arms around her waist and flipped them around so that she was the one leaning against the wall, while his arms rested on either side of her, trapping her within. His biceps flexed as he resisted touching her. He leaned his forehead against hers. 'We need to wait. This isn't the right time.' He stepped away and walked into the living room.

Maree followed. She grabbed his arm and pulled him to stop. 'I know what I want.'

She held his hand, while he kept his body facing away from her. All he had to do was shrug her hand away, but he couldn't do it.

'Maree, I don't think this is a good idea.'

'Why?' She squeezed his hand.

'I don't want to catch you on the rebound.'

'I'm not on the rebound,' Maree said.

'You're not?' Tom turned and looked at her.

'I was heartbroken after it ended, but lately I've been thinking. He didn't fight for us, and really, that says it all. He should have trusted me to try to forgive him.'

'Do you mean that?' Tom asked, his heart speeding up. 'Do you think you could have forgiven him for lying to you?'

'I could have tried, but it doesn't matter anymore. Our moment has passed and I want something else,' Maree whispered, bringing her hands to his face and searching his eyes.

Tom knew he should walk away right now, but he was helpless under the caress of her fingers. His head was spinning with her revelation that she might have been able to forgive Beau. Had he made a monumental mistake in not trusting her?

She leaned in and pressed her lips against his. Her kiss was ravenous with need. She pushed him onto the armchair and sat on his lap, her thighs gripping his sides. Her breasts pressed against his chest and made him moan with need. She was kissing him with abandon and he lost himself to her, the feel of her soft skin, holding her hair in his hand as he ravished her lips. Maree began undoing the buttons on his shirt.

'We've got to stop,' he said, taking her hands in his.

'I don't want to stop,' she whispered against his neck. 'I just want to be with you.'

'No, no.' Tom became more forceful, holding both her wrists with one hand and cupping her face with the other. 'Not like this. When we make love I want to know that you want me. That you're making that decision because you want me and only me.'

'But I do,' Maree said. 'I want you.'

'Then we can wait,' Tom said, getting up and lifting her with him. 'Now you have to go to bed.' He led her into her bedroom and went to close the door on her.

'Where are you going?' Maree asked.

'To have a cold shower,' he said gruffly and left.

Chapter 18

After Tom left to have a shower, Maree stood in the middle of the living room feeling bereft. She knew what he was saying made sense. After her failed romance with Beau she needed to protect her heart and make sure that what they had was real and true, before jumping in again. But there was this part of her that was sick of waiting, and tired of caution. She just wanted to feel. She wanted to make love with the man she loved. Maree nearly gasped, her hand covering her mouth. She was overcome with a wave of dizziness and had to sit down. Did she really just think that? She waited for her rational side to pipe up with logic—it was too soon, their love was untested—but none of these rang true. Her feelings were real and, moreover, she was sure Tom felt the same. She remembered again the way he had thrown himself in front of a car for her and the look of terror on his face. He loved her. She couldn't wait any longer. She had to be with him.

Maree walked into the bathroom and pulled the shower curtain away. Tom was standing under the shower, his forehead pressed against the cold tiles. He lifted his head and looked at her.

'Maree,' he pleaded.

She could see the strain he was under in trying to resist her and do the right thing. Any doubts she had melted away. They were meant to be together.

She stepped into the shower and kissed him. He held himself back for a moment, before wrapping his arms around her. She wanted to be closer to him and took off her shirt. Tom undid the snap off her cut-offs and she stepped out of them.

She felt such a sense of deja vu as if they had kissed like this in another lifetime. Her hands moved over his face, down his jaw and onto his chest. Something felt wrong. She broke the kiss and looked up at him. The water was dripping down his face and with his hair slicked back, he looked familiar. The cheekbones, the shape of his jaw, all reminded her of ...

'Beau?' she whispered, looking at him with confusion.

Time slowed as she waited for Tom's response.

He nodded imperceptibly.

Her head was spinning as she tried to process what she was seeing. She felt so dizzy and could barely stand on her feet. Her eyes blurred and suddenly there were two of them in the shower, both Tom and Beau were standing side by side. Fear hit her. She was going crazy and seeing things that weren't there. She stumbled out of the shower, pulling a towel around herself.

'I don't understand,' she said.

'I'm so sorry,' Tom said as he grabbed a towel and wrapped it around his torso. 'I wanted to tell you, but there was never the right moment.'

She turned to look at him. 'You were Beau and Tom,' she said, still in disbelief.

'Yes,' he said.

She turned away as the pieces began falling into place. The way Tom was so persistent in seeing her after they met for the first time, the easy familiarity they had with each other as soon as they met, and most importantly, how strong her feelings were for him. No wonder she had fallen in love with him so effortlessly. She had never stopped loving him.

'But why? Why would you play such a trick on me?' she asked.

'I didn't mean to. I was in character as research when I met you. When we went on a date I realized I was falling for you, but it was too late by then. You knew me as Beau, and I knew I'd made the biggest mistake of my life.'

Maree remembered the first time she saw him. She had felt a connection that was stronger than anything she'd felt before. Beau had told her that they couldn't see each other again, and she had thought it was because of her past. He'd come in to her house after their date to explain why and she had found him crying. That must have been the moment that he realized what he had done.

Her thoughts were whirling. Her emotions battered her as if she was inside a tornado. She needed space. She walked into the bedroom and threw herself across the bed as she tried to make sense of it all, but her head was still spinning.

The bed dipped as Tom sat next to her, bringing her back to the present.

'I'm so sorry,' he said. 'I never wanted to hurt you. It just happened. I never stopped fighting for you. Everything I have done has been to be with you.'

Maree realized he was telling the truth. He had done every-thing he could for them to be together, and he had tried to resist making love to her—she was the one who didn't want to wait.

She turned to look at him. Rivulets of water trailed down his torso and soaked into the towel around his waist. 'Why didn't you tell me the truth?'

He frowned as he raked his hand through his hair. 'I was scared. I thought that if I told you straight away you'd never want to speak to me again. You said you would never date an actor, so I thought I had to win you over first, convince you I was different, and then I would tell you. But then ...' He sighed deeply. '... things happened, and I tried, but it was never the right time.'

Maree remembered their lunch date before the stalker at-tacked. He'd said he wanted to tell her something. She sat up and looked him in the face. 'I can't believe it was you. It was always you.'

He cupped her cheek. 'You're not angry?'

There was a part of her that realized something was off with her reaction. She should be furious that he hadn't trusted her, or their love, and he'd put them both through hell as a result, but that voice was drowned out. Everything that was happening felt slightly unreal and dreamlike. She was so relieved that she hadn't made a mistake in giving her heart to a man who had abandoned her. Her instincts had been right all along. She had been so heartbroken when Beau left her without fighting for them, but now she realized that Tom had been fighting all along. He'd never left her. He loved her just as much as she loved him.

She shook her head, disbelieving what she saw before her eyes. Was this a dream? 'You came back to me. You didn't leave me.' Her hands reached for his face and she traced his features with her fingertips.

'I'll never leave you. I will always fight for you.'

He hugged her and she drew her arms around his neck, just enjoying the feel of him. She couldn't believe that she'd found the love of her life and he felt exactly the same way.

'I love you, Maree.' He kissed her.

She teared up, hearing the words she had been so desperate for. Their kiss was tender, almost chaste, but it didn't take long for the passion between them to heat up. He pulled her onto his lap, the towel falling away and she could feel his erection against her silk panties.

He kissed his way down her neck and to her breasts. He unhooked her bra and cupped her breasts in his hands. 'You are so beautiful,' he whispered as he worshipped her.

He was trying to savor her, but she wanted him now. She pushed him down so he was lying on his back. She admired his taut chest, her fingers gently brushing over the graze. He was so beautifully built. Her hands caressed him, loving the feeling of his hard muscles under her hands. She bent and kissed her way down his chest, her hands closing over his erection.

He groaned, the primal sound making her blood heat up. She couldn't wait any longer. She stood up, loving the way he watched her as she pulled down her panties. His hands clenched the bedspread, as if he was holding himself in check. She felt gratified to see the way he was fighting for control. She kneeled over him, her thighs on each side of his hips, and took him inside her in one hard thrust. Her head fell back as she let out a moan. She wanted more. She rode him hard, each thrust bringing her closer and closer.

She came first, the force of her orgasm wrenching a scream from her. He kept thrusting and she rode the waves of pleasure. He tensed under her as he came, his arms squeezing her tight, their chests pressed against each other. She felt his racing heart against hers and smiled with satisfaction. She lay down and placed her head on his chest.

Tom covered them with the duvet.

'I love you, Maree,' he whispered against her shoulder and fell asleep.

'I love you, Tom.' She fell asleep wearing a smile.

·❤·❤·❤·❤·❤·

Tom looked at Maree's sleeping face. He felt complete. He couldn't believe that all his fears came to nothing and that she was able to forgive him. He was angry with himself for not trusting her with the truth and for all the time they had lost. He kissed her shoulder. He promised himself he wouldn't let anything else stand in their way. From now on he had to be truthful. As soon as she woke up he'd talk to her about the stalker and tell her how close they were to capturing her.

He fell asleep with Maree on his shoulder, her leg curled over his thigh, her arm across his chest, her hand cupping his neck. He woke up sometime later, an odd sound disrupting his sleep.

He opened his eyes and stared at the ceiling, trying to place it. He looked down at Maree. She was panting slightly in her sleep.

'Maree.' He tried to rouse her awake. She opened her eyes, but seemed to look through him. He put his hand on her cheek. She was hot to his touch.

'That's lovely.' She held his hand to her forehead.

'Are you all right?' Tom lifted himself on his elbow beside her. 'You're burning up.'

'I am. Ouch.' She winced, holding her ear. 'Oh no. I think I've got an ear infection.' Her head drooped and she leaned against him. 'I'm so tired.' She gazed up at him with her big, brown eyes, looking so vulnerable and in pain.

'I'll go check the medicine cabinet,' he said.

He found some aspirin. He brought it back to her with a glass of water and she drank it down. She was still hot. Her breath was coming in pants and she had kicked off the covers.

Tom went to the front door and called out to Tony. 'We need a doctor,' he said. 'Maree is sick.'

'Carter told us we couldn't leave the property,' Tony said.

'Carter can jump. Maree needs a doctor and you need to bring one to her.'

Tom found his phone and called Carter.

'It's best if you stay there and out of harm's way,' Carter told him when he explained what was going on. 'I'll get Diane to come to you. Is that going to be a problem?'

Diane was one of the few people who knew his secret. She was the doctor who'd given him the pressure point injections as Beau.

'It's fine. I told Maree the truth and she forgave me.' A smile broke out on Tom's face. He still couldn't believe he was so lucky, that he'd spent all these months worrying what would happen when Maree found out, and in the end it didn't matter. He'd been such a fool not to trust her earlier.

'She did?' Carter's voice was full of surprise. 'That's great. I'm happy for you.'

After Tom hung up he went to check on Maree. Her forehead was still hot. He wet a washcloth and placed it on her forehead.

'The doctor is on her way,' he said, when she stirred and opened her eyes.

'What time is it?'

He looked at the clock. 'It's ten o'clock. Do you want some tea?'

She nodded.

He went to the kitchen and made her tea. He returned and handed her the cup. 'It's chamomile and honey.'

Maree took a few sips, but she struggled to hold her head up. He sat beside her and let her lean against him as she drank. When she finished, Tom put the cup on the bedside table and helped her lie down. As he waited for the doctor to arrive, he placed wet compresses on her forehead while she slept fitfully.

An hour later there was a knock at the door. Tom opened it and let in Carter and Diane.

'Thanks for coming out all this way,' Tom said to Diane.

'That's all right,' she said. 'The incentive is quite substantial.' She glanced at Carter.

Tom made a mental note to repay Carter the fee.

'This is a beautiful cottage ,' Diane said. 'Such a shame your romantic getaway has been marred by illness.'

'I don't care. I just want Maree to be okay.'

'Oh, dear, has the playboy been tamed?' she asked wryly.

Tom remembered that Diane had seen him at his most depraved. He hated being reminded of that period of his life. 'Maree is special.'

Diane forced a smile. 'I'm happy for you. So where is my patient?'

'She's in the bedroom.' Tom walked through the living room and Diane followed. He opened the bedroom door. 'Maree, the doctor is here,' he said. He entered and went to the bed, helping Maree sit up.

Carter waited in the doorway while Diane entered.

'Maree this is Dr Diane—' He hesitated as he realized he didn't remember her surname.

Diane's face creased with annoyance. 'I'm Dr Collins. What seems to be the problem?'

'I think I've got an ear infection,' Maree said.

Diane opened her bag and took out a tongue depressor. She examined Maree's throat then took out an otoscope and looked into Maree's ears. 'Definitely an ear infection. I'll give you a shot of penicillin and then write a prescription that you can fill tomorrow. You should leave so we have privacy.' Diane nodded at Tom and Carter.

'Didn't you say you were out of penicillin in the car?' Carter said. 'Just write a prescription and I'll have Tony go and fill it.'

Diane hesitated, staring at Carter. 'That's right. I'll just leave a prescription.' She and Carter left the bedroom.

Maree wilted in Tom's arms. He covered her with the duvet and followed the others out. Diane handed him a prescription. 'Here. This should do the trick. It's important she keeps hydrated,' said Diane. 'I just need to wash my hands.'

Tom pointed down the hall. 'Second on the left.'

Diane nodded and walked down the hall.

'Is there any news about the stalker?' he asked Carter.

'We've lifted a fingerprint from the last note,' Carter said. 'It was only a matter of time until the stalker got sloppy. The police are running it and we'll have the identity in a couple of days.'

'Good.' Tom rifled his hand through his hair. 'I want my life back and I want the person responsible for all this madness in jail.'

'It will happen.' Carter slapped him on the shoulder. 'You're almost home free.'

Tom smiled, realizing he had a lot to be thankful for. He and Maree were together, regardless of what happened with the stalker.

Diane returned from the bathroom. She opened her bag and frowned. 'I think I've forgotten something in the room. I'll just be a sec.' She went back into Maree's bedroom and returned a moment later. 'I'm ready to go.' She turned at the door and offered her hand to Tom. 'Congratulations on the next chapter of your life. Hopefully it will be as exciting as your new movie.'

'I'm over excitement.' Tom said. 'I want life in the slow lane.'

Diane laughed, almost shrill. 'Be careful what you wish for.' She tapped him on the nose and walked into the darkness.

Tom looked at Carter.

'Sorry about that,' Carter said. 'She's going through a bit of a rough time and is under some strain.'

'What sort of strain?' Tom asked. Carter went to leave without answering. 'Wait a minute,' Tom demanded, getting suspicious. Carter had a habit of feigning deafness when he didn't want to answer certain questions. 'What is going on with Dr Collins?'

Carter rubbed his neck and looked away as he answered. 'Well, she's had her medical license revoked.'

'You had an unlicensed doctor inject me with drugs?' Tom demanded.

'No, God no,' Carter said. 'She still had her license then, this happened just a few days ago.'

'And you had her treat Maree anyway?'

'She told me while we were driving up here,' Carter said. 'I figured it couldn't hurt for her to examine Maree.'

'She wanted to inject her too,' Tom said, fury burning him up. He couldn't believe Tom had risked Maree's health in such a way.

'Yes, but I wasn't going to allow that to happen. Now I'm going to fax the prescription to the local 24-hour pharmacy where Tony can pick it up for you.' Carter took out his phone and started dialing.

'But can we trust Diane's diagnosis? We should get another doctor to examine her.'

Carter hesitated. 'Look, we can do that, but a course of antibiotics in the meantime won't hurt.'

Tom nodded. 'Okay, but I want a second opinion first thing tomorrow morning.'

Carter nodded. 'I'll make the arrangements.'

Tom waited in the doorway until the headlights disappeared. He returned to the bedroom and found Maree deeply asleep. As he walked toward the bed he hit something with his foot and it bounced off the wall with a bang. Maree didn't stir. He knelt down on the floor and checked under the bed. He saw something shiny glinting and pulled it out. It was Maree's cell phone. He returned it to the bedside table and then lay down beside her.

Chapter 19

When Maree woke up she didn't where she was. The ceiling above her with its wooden beams was unfamiliar. She sat up in bed and looked out the window to the forest. Slowly images came back—Tom, the cabin, the stalker.

She lay back down, collecting her energy for a moment. All her muscles ached, and her head felt slightly floaty. Feeling the press of her bladder she pushed the covers off and swung her feet out of bed. Her toes curled as they hit the cold floor. She started walking toward the bathroom, the wooden floor creaking beneath her bare feet. She felt so strange, her head ached as if she had a hangover yet she'd only had one glass of wine with dinner. She looked in the mirror above the vanity. Her hair was tousled, and there were dark circles under her eyes. She washed her face and ran a brush through her hair.

When she returned to bed, the door opened and Tom appeared.

'You're up.' He smiled as he came in. 'How are you feeling?'

'Okay.' Maree held onto the bed post as her energy deserted her.

'Here, let me help you.' Tom stepped forward, helping her back to bed. He sat on the edge, smoothing her hair off her face.

'You had me worried there for a while, but the fever broke a few hours ago.'

'Fever?' Maree asked.

'Yes, you had an infection.'

Maree remembered feeling hot the night before. Her head had felt fuzzy and everything was out of focus. She'd thought it was the humidity.

'You started improving after you started the antibiotics yesterday.'

'What antibiotics?' Maree asked, feeling confused.

'Carter's doctor came to see you yesterday morning. He gave you a penicillin injection.'

'I thought the doctor was a woman,' Maree asked, having a vague memory of a blonde woman examining her.

'Diane came first, but she didn't have the medication you needed so we called someone else. What do you remember?' Tom asked.

'I remember us having dinner. And then everything gets a little blurred.'

She remembered that she came onto him, desperately wanting to get him into bed, and that he'd rebuffed her. He'd said that he wanted to wait, and while she knew that he had concerns about her feelings for Beau, for a moment she wondered if he was just not that into her, but something within her refused to believe it. She'd seen the attraction in his eyes when he looked at her. There was another reason he was holding back.

'That's not the last thing you remember?'

'Why? Did something happen after that?'

Tom laughed. 'Nice. You almost got me.'

Maree looked at him in confusion.

Tom's face dropped. 'Are you serious? You don't remember?'

'You're scaring me,' Maree said. 'I'm starting to think I did something embarrassing.'

Tom looked down. 'Nothing too embarrassing. I'll get breakfast.'

After he left she lay back down. Even the short conversation had exhausted her. She didn't know if she had the energy to eat. She closed her eyes and drifted, listening to the sound of pots and pans as Tom cooked.

In her dream Tom held himself above her as they kissed. She stroked his back, loving every smooth inch of his skin. He moved down her body, kissing her all over. She rolled him onto his back and sat on top of him, loving the feel of his skin under hers.

'Maree, Maree,' he called her name, his voice husky with desire.

She opened her eyes, fighting to force the eyelids back. Tom was standing by the bed holding a tray.

'I'm sorry for waking you, but you need to eat something to build your strength up.'

Maree flushed as she sat up. She couldn't believe that she was having erotic dreams about him. Was she fifteen years old?

Tom placed the tray on her lap. He'd made her an omelette and tea, with thick sliced fresh bread and orange juice. Maree ate slowly. She felt her strength returning.

Tom seemed preoccupied. 'Is something wrong?' Maree asked.

'I'm just a little worried that you don't remember the doctor visiting,' Tom said.

Maree frowned. 'It's probably because I had such a high fever. I was feeling a bit off all day, but I didn't realize what was happening.'

'Has that happened before?' Tom asked.

Maree frowned. While she'd had ear infections before, she'd never had the experience of losing time. 'No, it hasn't.'

At least now she knew why she'd been so lust-struck. The fever had been working through her body, lowering her inhibitions and making her act out of character. Thankfully Tom had the foresight to resist until she was sure of her emotions before they took their relationship to the next level.

'You look worried,' she said. 'Is something wrong?'

Tom shook his head. 'Of course not.' But he didn't meet her eyes.

Maree felt a sense of wrongness. She knew he was lying to her, but she didn't have the energy to confront him.

'I'll leave you to rest.' He picked up the tray and left the bedroom.

She lay back and, even though she wanted to figure out what was going on with Tom, exhaustion overwhelmed her and she fell asleep again.

A beeping sound woke her up. It took a moment for sleep to clear and for her to recognize the sound as her cell phone. She'd received a text. She reached for the phone on the bedside table and looked at the screen. When she saw Beau's name her stomach dropped. She was about to open the message, but hesitated. Did she really want to read it?

She'd spent so many weeks desperate for news from Beau. All she'd wanted was to see him, to talk to him, to convince him that they belonged together, but now she was confused. Her relationship with Beau felt so far away, it was like another lifetime and she'd been another person. She didn't know if she wanted to revisit that time in her life.

She remembered her last conversation with Tom. While they had dinner last night on the porch she'd felt his gaze on her and knew he was attracted to her, and yet when she'd come onto him he'd wanted to wait for her to be sure before they made love. Any other man in that situation wouldn't have hesitated to be with her, but he didn't. He'd said he wanted to be more than a one night stand and that she had to make sure she was over Beau.

She'd tried to convince him that Beau was in her past, but was he really? Even though she'd tried to forget about him and move on with her life, she realized there was still an ache there. Beau had whirled through her life, smashed her defenses and then left her heartbroken. While her feelings for Tom were much stronger, there was still an element of unfinished business between her and Beau.

Maree opened the message.

'Dear Maree, I'm sorry I ran away without explanation. Please give me a chance to tell you why I had to leave. Yours always, Beau.'

Anger burned through her. How dare he? He'd had his chance and he'd blown it. She didn't owe him anything. She started typing a reply, but quickly took a deep breath. 'Don't text angry,' she told herself. It was a sentence she'd had occasion to repeat more than once to Allegra, whose hot-tempered impulses had led to many subsequent apologies.

She remembered Beau's brown eyes and bearded face and a tenderness filled her. She still had feelings for him, but they were muted now by the feelings she'd developed for Tom. The two men were so different on the surface, yet so alike in all the ways that mattered. They both tugged at her heartstrings. Tom had told her he wanted her to be sure of her feelings before they went any further with their relationship, yet here she was having received one text message, and she was instantly jumbled and confused. Maybe she owed it to Tom to see Beau and get closure? To make sure that Beau was in her past so that Tom could be in her future?

She was about to type a reply when Tom came into her room. 'We have to return to LA.'

Chapter 20

Tom closed the door to Maree's bedroom. He felt shaken. As he'd prepared breakfast earlier, he'd tried to understand why Maree couldn't remember their night together. He realized now that she'd been acting out character the night before. She had been so amorous, and like a fool he had been too flattered to sense why. He'd been so focused on making sure that he didn't give into temptation that it hadn't occurred to him to wonder whether everything was all right with her.

On reflection, he realized she had felt warm to his touch; still, her fever couldn't have been that high or he would have noticed. It was only during the night that it had spiked and it had become obvious that she was ill. He saw the wineglasses on the dish rack. Did she drink too much? He'd had a glass of wine and he didn't remember Maree refilling her glass, but perhaps she'd had a few drinks while he was sleeping.

Tom had made her an omelette and served it, taking the opportunity to question her further. Her admission that she'd never forgotten things before while suffering from a fever made an internal alarm go off. He'd left her room, thoughts swirling around his head, when there was a knock on the door.

When he opened it, he found Tony holding Norman Keller by the jacket. 'I found this one circling the perimeter,' Tony said. 'Do you want me to call the police?'

Tom hesitated. If he pressed charges against Norman for trespassing it guaranteed that he would be harassed by other paparazzi who would close ranks to protect one of their own. Still, maybe this was his chance to gain the upper hand and finally find out how Norman knew his every move.

'Tell me how you found me and I won't call the police and press trespassing charges,' Tom said. He'd expected Norman to look nervous, but Norman's face creased with annoyance.

'Come on, Calvert, enough with the histrionics,' Norman said.

'What the hell are you talking about?' Tom demanded.

'I don't know what game you and Carter are playing, but you can't press charges against me when I'm an invited guest.'

Norman went for his pocket, and Tony reached forward and held his arm.

'Relax,' Norman said. 'I'm just getting out my cell phone.'

Tony released his arm. Norman fished out his phone and pressed a few buttons. He handed Tom the phone. Tom read the message—it was the cabin's address.

'Who sent this to you?' Tom grabbed Norman's shirt.

'Don't play dumb. I'm sure you have your agent's number memorized.'

Tom felt like he was breathing underwater. He took out his phone and compared the numbers; it was definitely Carter's. He checked the time stamp. It was sent at midnight, after Carter had brought Diane over.

'This doesn't make sense,' Tom said to himself.

'Of course it does. Carter knows how the game is played, even if you don't.' Norman was smirking as he snatched back his phone. 'He's been feeding me your whereabouts so you get prime tabloid inches. We all know how it works. More publicity equals a box office hit.'

'That's bullshit.' Tom went to grab Norman again, but Norman ducked behind Tony.

'Hey, I'm just giving you the truth,' he said. 'Don't shoot the messenger.'

Tom started going after him, but Tony stepped in and held him back. Norman turned and ran down the driveway. Tom felt dazed and thick-headed. Was it really true? Could Carter have betrayed him like this? He knew his agent was ruthless in his ambition, that was one of his best features. When he believed in his client Carter would move heaven and earth to make a project happen. He'd always encouraged Tom to play the game and be out and about at the customary premieres and industry dos, but Carter would have no reason to go behind his back. When he wanted Tom to do something, he just strong-armed him into it using logic and persuasion. He had no reason to be manipulative.

On the other hand, Norman had every reason to lie. His whole career was based on being underhanded and sneaky. The only way he could get the exclusives he did was by grooming informants who were on his payroll. But that didn't explain why Norman had a message from Carter's number.

'Should I chase after him?' Tony asked.

Tom shook his head. Norman wasn't important right now. 'We have to pack up and leave.'

Their safe haven was compromised. If Norman knew where they were it was only a matter of time before other paparazzi descended.

'You don't believe anything that guy said, do you?' Tony asked.

'No, but I have to get back to the city and have a conversation with Carter.' Tom met Tony's eyes. 'I know Carter throws a lot of work your way and you want to give him the heads up, but you signed a confidentiality agreement when you were given this detail, so this conversation doesn't go any further.'

'But you know that Carter didn't—'

'I don't know anything right now,' Tom snapped. 'Except that if you tell Carter what Norman said you won't be hired by another security firm again.'

Tony looked chastened. 'I still have to tell Carter that we're leaving.'

'Tell him that and nothing more. I'll go tell Maree while you tell Ross we have to leave.' Tom watched Tony go down the porch stairs. He felt guilty at having to stonewall Tony, but the only way he was going to find out the truth was if Carter didn't know he was coming.

Tom walked into Maree's room and got her suitcase. 'We have to return to LA.'

'Why?' she asked.

'The paparazzi have found us.' Tom removed her clothes from the wardrobe and started packing them into the suitcase.

'How?' she persisted.

'That's what I need to find out.' Noticing her worried face, he stopped what he was doing. 'It's going to be okay.' He came over and cupped her cheek. 'We'll check into a hotel, and Ross and Tony will stay with us until we find out who the stalker is. The police have a fingerprint and should know today.'

Maree nodded and moved away. She took her jeans out of the suitcase. 'I think I'll stay with Allegra.'

He drew his breath in sharply. She was backing away from him.

'I have to get back on track with the costume designs and she has a home office.'

'Of course.' Tom nodded.

On the surface her excuse sounded perfectly plausible, but he noticed her preoccupied air and the way she avoided his touch. He felt a cold chill. She'd changed her mind about them. He took a deep breath. Now wasn't the time to dwell on it. First he needed to make sure she was safe, then he had to find a way to finally tell her the truth, again. If she couldn't forgive him he'd just have to work to change her mind. He knew that they belonged together and he wasn't going to give up without a fight.

'I'll go pack,' he said.

Tom was zipping up his suitcase in his room when his phone rang. Seeing Carter's name on the screen he hesitated about picking up. He wanted to talk to him face to face about Norman's accusations, but Carter might have heard from the police about the stalker's identity.

'Still no news,' Carter said, pre-empting Tom's query. 'Tony called me. He said you had a visitor.'

'Yes. We're just leaving now. I'm going to drop Maree off at Allegra's house and then I'll come to the office.'

'Okay,' Carter said. 'See you then.'

Tom came into the living room where Maree was waiting by the front door. He picked up her suitcase and carried it to the car. She walked slowly. Her face looked wan and she was still obviously exhausted. They sat together in the backseat and soon after they left, Maree's head dropped onto his shoulder and she fell asleep. He gently caressed her hair, tenderness filling him. He hated that her life was so unsettled. He decided that regardless of whether the stalker was found today or not, he had to tell Maree the truth, including the fact that they had made love the night before. But first he had to deal with Carter.

When they arrived at Allegra's an hour later, Tom nudged Maree awake. She opened her eyes and her lips curved into a smile. 'Hello,' she said, leaning forward for a kiss.

'We're here,' Tom said, forestalling her as he nodded out the window.

She turned to look and saw Allegra's house.

'Oh, of course.'

He felt momentarily deflated. He wished he could have just let her lips sink effortlessly into his, but he would just feel like a jerk if he accepted her affection while there were still so many lies between them. Tom got Maree's suitcase from the trunk, while Tony unlocked the front door and went to check the premises.

'I have to see Carter about something,' Tom said, as he walked Maree up to the front door. 'As soon as I'm finished I'll come right back.' He took her hands in his. 'There is so much I need to tell you, so much you need to know, but the one thing I don't want you to forget is that I—'

He cut himself off. He couldn't tell her that he loved her. He couldn't make that mistake again and manipulate her into admitting her feelings when she still didn't know the truth.

'... I care about you,' he said finally, stumbling as he tried to find the words. 'I care about you a lot.'

Maree frowned and he felt like a heel. Once again he'd botched it. He just couldn't do anything right.

But Maree was smiling. 'I care about you too. And you're right, we do need to talk. I'll be waiting.'

Relief filled him. He touched his forehead to hers. He wanted to kiss her, but this was the only contact he would permit himself.

Tony returned. 'It's all clear,' he said.

Tom nodded.

'I guess I'll see you soon.' Maree stepped inside.

'See you,' Tom said.

He walked back to the car and got in the passenger seat. 'Take me to Carter's office,' he told Ross.

He found his agent in his office. It was the end of the day and most the offices were empty, the lights turned off, plunging the floor into darkness. Carter was sitting on the sofa drinking Scotch, a script in his hand.

'There's my favorite client.' He smiled and put the script on the table. 'What's your poison?' he asked as he went to the bar and picked up a glass.

'Nothing, thanks.'

'What's the matter?' Carter put the glass down and looked at him with concern.

'I heard some disturbing news from Norman today.'

'What did that weasel say?' Carter sat back down and sipped his Scotch.

'He said that you were the source who leaked the whereabouts of the cabin.'

Carter let out a bark of laughter. 'That slimy little man. What angle is he playing at?'

'That's what I was wondering,' Tom said. 'But then he showed me the message he received. Can I have your phone?'

'My phone?' Carter quirked an eyebrow.

'Yes, please.' Tom didn't expect the message to be there, after all Carter had time to delete the incriminating text, but he was hoping to find something that would explain what happened. He flicked to the sent message folder and hesitated. It was there. He turned the screen toward Carter and showed him the message.

Carter was mid-sip and he spluttered, the Scotch spraying all over the table. 'What the fuck?' Carter took the phone from him and looked closer. 'I've never seen this message before.'

Tom didn't know what to believe. The evidence was there, the truth was staring him in the face. Carter was the one who had betrayed him.

'You've got to believe me, bro,' Carter said. 'You know I'd never betray you like this.'

'I don't know what to believe.' Tom rubbed his hands down his face.

Carter stood and started pacing. 'Well, there's one thing you can believe. You know I'm all about the business and, our friendship aside, you know I'd never fuck a client and risk losing a pay check.'

Tom hesitated. He knew the truth when he heard it. Carter was a shark. When he scented he was about to make money he wouldn't do anything to jeopardize it. While no one knew yet that Tom was the lead role in *Heroes in Tennessee*, one fact was unavoidable—Ken Grey was a gold-plated director and any movie he made would be the talk of Tinseltown, which meant that Tom was about to hit the big time. Carter wouldn't risk their relationship now.

'Well, then you tell me what the hell happened,' said Tom. 'Did someone steal your cell phone?'

'No, no. It's been with me every minute. You know how attached I am to that thing.'

Carter's cell phone was his lifeline and he had it with him constantly; even when he was supposedly relaxing, it was always a second's reach from his hand.

'Did anyone else use it at all?' Tom asked.

Someone had to be the leak, and there were only a few people who knew about them being at the cabin—Allegra, Tony and Ross, Carter, and Diane.

'While we were driving up back from the cabin Diane had to use my phone because her battery was dead.' Carter shrugged. 'But that's the only time.'

Tom felt a chill settle over him.

'What are you thinking?' Carter stopped pacing. 'It can't be Diane. Why would she do that?'

Tom felt the fogginess of memory lift. He remembered when he'd met Diane the first time. It was at Carter's New Year's Eve party. His career was taking a nosedive after his arrest and he'd thought he'd never get another job. He'd been drinking heavily the previous few months, and on this night he was drunk before he even arrived at Carter's house, and then he kept drinking.

There was a blonde in a red dress. She was sweet and nervous as she approached him and told him she was a fan and that she'd loved his latest movie, a piece of crap Tom had phoned in. They started talking and he flirted as usual and she flirted back. So he asked her to go upstairs. She hesitated for a moment and then nodded. They had perfunctory sex, and afterward she gave him her number and he promised he would call. He promptly forgot about her.

'I think I know why,' Tom said. 'We had a one night stand at the New Year's party.'

'Shit,' Carter exclaimed. 'Her marriage ended because her husband found out she cheated. Soon after that she developed problems at work and got fired, and as you know, she just lost her license because of malpractice. I'll call the police,' Carter said and picked up his phone.

While Carter talked to the police Tom received a text from Maree and smiled. His smile quickly faded when he opened the message.

'This is you know who. I have your little friend here and she's waiting for you. Don't disappoint her or there will be a price to pay. If I see the cops, she dies.'

There was a photo attached. Maree was sitting in an armchair, her eyes wide with fear as the photo was taken. Tom felt his stomach drop. *Oh God, he was too late.*

'Well, you were right,' Carter said behind him. 'The police have identified the fingerprint. It's Diane's. They're going to her house to pick her up.'

Tom closed the message and returned the phone to his pocket. If Carter knew about the message he would insist on involving the police. His first priority would be to ensure Tom's safety, even if it meant putting Maree in danger. Tom was on his own. There was only one thing he could do. He had to meet Diane's demand.

'What's wrong?' Carter demanded.

'Nothing.' Tom forced a smile. 'It's a message from Maree. I'd better get going.' He started for the door.

'Wait,' Carter called.

Tom paused. *Shit, Carter had figured it out.* Tom clenched his fist as he readied himself for a showdown. He wasn't going to let anyone stop him from saving Maree. He turned around.

'Listen, bro, it meant a lot that you believed me even before you had proof.' Carter was looking at the ground as he spoke, his mouth forming a crooked smile. 'I don't have too many real friends, this business doesn't allow it. But I'm glad I've got you on my side.'

Tom hesitated. He knew how much it cost Carter to say that. He wasn't known for sentimentality. 'Always.' Tom offered his hand.

Carter took it, pulling him into a quick hug.

Tom barely had the chance to hug him back when Carter pulled away again. Carter returned to the couch and picked up the script. 'Don't you have some wooing to do?'

Tom nodded and left. He paused in the doorway. 'I'm glad I've got you on my side too.' He didn't turn around to see Carter's reaction.

Chapter 21

As Maree waited for a knock on the door she'd practiced her speech. Beau was due any minute now and she was nervous as hell. She had replied to Beau's message and asked him to meet her at Allegra's house. She'd realized on the drive back to Los Angeles what she had to tell Beau. She loved Tom and he was her future. She and Beau had a moment together. They could have had something, but Beau made the choice to leave, and that stopped whatever could have happened in its tracks.

She'd thought about calling Beau and telling him over the phone, but that felt tacky. She had to tell him in person. Even though she didn't owe Beau anything—he was the one who'd left the Dear Jane letter—she felt that they both needed some closure.

Maree checked her phone for the umpteenth time. She'd left a message for Allegra. She was the break-up queen—if anyone was going to have advice about how to perform such a delicate task, Allegra was the one.

There was a knock on the door and her heart started racing. Beau was early. She wasn't ready. 'Just a minute,' she said. She quickly checked her face in the mirror and smoothed back her hair, before opening the door.

She was nonplussed to find a woman standing in her doorway. It took her a moment to place her as Diane, the doctor who had seen her while she was sick at the cabin.

'Hello,' Diane said with a smile. 'I was just coming by to do a quick check of your vital signs. Carter gave me your address. I hope it's all right?'

Maree looked at Ross sitting in his car across the street. She had told him she needed privacy for a visitor so he was keeping watch from afar. She waved at him to let him know it was okay.

'Sure.' Maree held the door open for Diane to enter. 'I'm just expecting someone.'

'This won't take long,' Diane said as she entered. 'Nice place.'

'It's not mine.' Maree closed the front door. 'This is my friend's house.'

Maree's phone rang. She looked at the screen and saw it was Allegra. 'Excuse me a minute. I just have to take this.' She walked into the kitchen and answered. 'Allegra, what took you so long?'

'Something came up,' Allegra said archly.

It didn't take a genius to see through Allegra's double entendre.

'I need your advice.' Maree quickly told her about Beau's message. 'So now I have to tell him that I'm in love with someone else and his moment has passed and I don't know how to say it.'

'You're overcomplicating the situation,' Allegra said. 'Just listen to his side of the story, tell him how you feel and then show him out,' she sighed. 'I have to go. Something is coming up again.'

Maree turned around and found Diane standing in the doorway, listening. 'Sorry about that. Where were we?'

'I was just going to say how it must have been horrible to find your home being vandalized in such a manner.'

'I didn't tell you that my home was vandalized.' Maree's skin broke out in goosepimples as uneasiness gripped her.

'That's right, you didn't.' Diane smiled, but it didn't reach her eyes.

'My friend is going to be here any minute,' Maree said, her uneasiness becoming fear.

'No, he's not,' Diane said. Something in the dead way she spoke sent cold shivers down Maree's spine. Diane put her hand in her pocket and took out a gun.

'It's you,' Maree said, putting the pieces together. 'You're Tom's stalker.'

'Surprise.' Diane's mouth formed an empty smile.

'What do you want?'

'I want to help you,' Diane said.

'Help me? How?' Maree asked, feeling confused.

'Let's just say I want to save you from the same mistake I made. Give me your phone.'

Maree got out her cell phone.

Diane indicated with her gun that she should put it on the table. 'Now sit down.'

After Maree sat, Diane took a photo of her and then used her phone to send a message.

'Who are you sending that to?'

Diane smiled. 'It's a special message to your boyfriend.'

Maree realized that Tom was on his way. She could only hope that he would call the police and arrive with the cavalry, but there was one person she had to take care of. She looked at the clock. Beau was due in five minutes.

'Please let me call my friend and tell him not to come,' Maree begged. 'He's got nothing to do with this.'

'Poor simple Maree,' Diane said, looking at her with a mixture of pity and amusement. 'You still don't know.'

'Don't know what?' Maree demanded.

'As they say in the movies, all will be revealed.' Diane waved her arm, making the gun dance menacingly in her hand. 'Let's talk while we're waiting. So why did you pick Tom? You pretend you're so virtuous and good, yet you kicked the handicapped man to the curb so you could be with the movie star.'

'How do you know about Beau?'

'I'm the one asking the questions,' Diane snapped. 'So why did you choose Tom over the fake soldier?'

'I didn't.'

'Don't play with me,' Diane said. 'I know everything, and if you don't start talking ...' She pointed the gun at Maree and waited a beat.

'It's not like that at all,' Maree said, feeling a stab of irrational guilt. She still felt like she was doing something wrong by choosing Tom. After all, she'd loved Beau first and thought he was the one, but then she'd changed her mind. It didn't speak much about her character. 'I love Tom. Beau chose to walk away from any chance we had.'

'Is that the way it works?' Diane asked. 'If someone walks away, that's it for you. You just say goodbye.'

Maree shifted uncomfortably in her seat. Diane's question hit a bit too close to home. She knew that's what it looked like to someone outside of the situation, but she could only go by the beat of her heart, and her heart belonged to Tom.

'Just like I suspected, you're nothing but a star fucker,' Diane said with a laugh.

'Says the woman who can only get a man by stalking him,' Maree spat out, angry at being treated like a moth that a cat was toying with before the kill.

'Don't be impudent.' Diane struck her in the forehead with the gun.

Maree fell to the floor, clutching her head. Everything was spinning around her and she couldn't stand up. Time passed in darkness.

There was a knock on the door. Diane prodded her with her foot. 'Get up. That's lover boy. Open the door.'

Maree struggled to her feet, holding onto the back of the sofa to stand upright.

'Hurry up.' Diane opened her handbag and pulled out her compact, fluffing her hair as she checked her reflection. 'Don't keep him waiting.'

Maree stumbled to the door and opened it. She was shocked to find Tom.

'Run,' she said to him.

His eyes widened when he saw her. She started to sway but he quickly caught her, drawing his arm around her and holding her up.

'Hello Tom,' Diane said. She was standing watching them, the gun casually held against her thigh. 'Do come in and shut the door behind you.'

'Diane, you don't have to do this,' he said. 'Just let Maree go and you and I can talk.'

'Talk.' Diane barked with laughter. 'You mean like how we talked after our night together?'

'Your night together?' Maree asked, trying to understand what was going on.

'First things first. Put her on the couch.' Diane gestured toward Maree.

Tom helped Maree over to the couch and she sat down.

'Now shall I tell her or will you?' Diane asked.

'Please, don't do this,' Tom said. 'This is between you and me.'

'Yes, it is, lover boy,' Diane said. 'Now tell her the truth or I'll shoot her right here, right now.' Her voice was unhinged and hysterical. She was a woman on the edge of losing control.

'I'm so sorry,' Tom said as he met Maree's eyes. 'Please forgive me.'

'Forgive you for what?' Maree asked.

'I am Beau,' Tom said.

'What do you mean?' Maree was confused. Her head was aching and she thought she heard wrong.

'Tell her what you did,' Diane demanded.

'I was practicing for my new movie when I met you,' Tom said. 'I was planning on going out on a date with you, just to practice being in character, but then things spiraled out of control. We spent the night talking and I felt something I hadn't felt before. I was trying to tell you that I was leaving town that night, but things happened.'

'You, you lied to me,' Maree said, trying to process his confession. 'You pretended to love me.'

'I never pretended that,' Tom said. 'I do love you. I fell in love with you as Beau, and then I tried to get you to fall in love with me. The real me. I told you all this the night you were getting sick.'

'What are you talking about?' Maree was confused. 'You didn't tell me anything.'

'Yes I did, but you don't remember because you had a high fever.'

Diane waved her gun. 'It looks like she doesn't believe you.' Diane put on a sad face. 'And how could she when you're a liar. You just use women and throw them away. You didn't even remember who I was when Carter called me to do a favor for his friend who was practicing method acting and wanted to be in character by having pressure point injections to numb him.'

Maree gasped, realizing that when she'd made love with Beau it had been Tom.

'When Carter called me, I knew straightaway that you were the friend he was talking about. As you know I'd kept a very close eye on you, but I wanted to see what would happen when we saw each other face to face. You looked at me like I was a stranger. You didn't even remember that we'd slept together,' Diane raised her voice. 'I was just an anonymous nobody to you. Someone that you used to fill a night.'

'I'm sorry,' Tom said. 'But I was a different person. That's when I was partying too much. I didn't mean to hurt you.'

'You ruined my marriage,' Diane was shouting now. 'You seduced me that night, made me feel special and important. You made me think that you cared, so when you said let's go upstairs, I just blindly followed you.'

'Wait,' Tom said. 'You never said you were married. If you told me, I never would have come onto you.'

'It doesn't matter.' Diane clutched her head, the gun pressed up against her cheek so that it left a red mark on her skin. 'It doesn't matter. It was you. You were the one who took me upstairs. You made me think I was something to you, and then you tossed me away. You're the one who ruined my life. When my husband found out he threw me out. Now he's married to my best friend and I'm all alone. I knew when I saw you that night, that it was my chance to get revenge. I followed you and saw you with her and I saw that you were doing the same thing to her that you did to me—discarding her once she'd served her purpose—and I wasn't going to let you get away with it.'

'You're the one who killed Carter's dog,' Tom said, putting the pieces together.

'Yes,' Diane smiled. 'That was me. I was trying to find your weak spot. I didn't realize you didn't love that dog, but then when I realized that Maree wasn't just another woman to keep your bed warm I knew I could get my revenge. I was going to take away what you loved.'

'That's why you tried to run me down,' Maree whispered.

'Yes,' Diane said. 'He has to pay for what he's done to every woman out there. The way he's used them and thrown them away. He ruined my marriage and took away my career. I had it all, and now I have nothing.' She aimed the gun toward Maree. 'I'm sorry, but this is the only way to make him pay.'

'No, don't,' Tom begged. 'Don't do this.'

'You really love her, don't you?' Diane said, glaring at him.

'Yes, yes I do,' Tom said, looking at Maree.

As she met his eyes, Maree saw the love shining there. Now it was so obvious that Tom and Beau were the same person. She now knew why Tom felt so familiar and why she was so comfortable around him. It was as if her heart had known the truth all along, even if her head hadn't.

'Then I'm sorry about this.' Diane pointed the gun at Tom.

'No,' Maree gasped, expecting the gun to go off.

'But I'm sure you agree this is the only way to make him suffer. Like I told you Tom, what goes around, comes around.' Diane turned the gun back on Maree.

Maree couldn't take her eyes off the barrel. Maree flinched when she saw a blur hurtling toward Diane.

It was Tom. He'd launched himself across the room and thrown himself on top of Diane. There was a scuffle and a gun shot went off. Tom stood up holding the gun, while Diane remained on the ground.

'Is she all right?' Maree gasped, looking at her lifeless body on the ground.

'She's fine,' Tom said. 'She hit her head on the sideboard when I landed on her, but she's still breathing.'

He carefully opened the chamber and took out the bullets, placing them in his pocket before putting the gun on the table. He coughed, and blood came out of his mouth. That's when Maree looked down and saw the blotch of red spreading across his midriff.

'Oh my God!' she cried, catching him as he fell. 'You've been shot.'

Ross burst through the door. 'What the?' he said as he saw Tom in Maree's arms. He quickly recovered and took out his cell phone and dialed 911.

Tom was becoming pale as the blood stain spread further.

'I'm so sorry,' Tom said as Maree held his head on her lap.

'Don't worry about that now.' She took off her cardigan and pressed it against the bullet wound. 'We'll talk about that later.'

Tom smiled sadly. 'There won't be a later. I want you to know that I love you. You're the only woman I've ever loved. You're the woman I imagined spending the rest of my life with.'

'Don't say this now.' Maree began to cry, realizing that she was losing the man she loved.

'I have to. This is the only moment I have to be with you. It's always been you, Maree.'

'I love you,' Maree gasped between breaths. 'I love you, Tom.'

He smiled. She leaned down and kissed him. Then he went limp.

'Tom.' She shook his shoulder. 'Tom!' she called again. She bent her head and there was no breath coming out of his nose. 'God, no, don't leave me now.' She placed his head on the floor and bent over him, giving him a quick breath in the mouth.

She started pumping his chest. The paramedics appeared at the door.

'Please help me,' she shouted frantically. 'He's not breathing.'

She moved out of the way and the paramedics took over CPR. The female paramedic did compressions on his chest while another got the defibrillator ready. After undoing his shirt they placed the paddles on his bare chest.

'Clear,' the female paramedic said and the man lifted his hands. She turned a switch and the defibrillator made a sound.

Tom's chest rose, but nothing happened.

'Again,' the female paramedic said and turned the knob. Tom's chest jumped up and this time a heartbeat appeared on the monitor.

Maree held his hand tightly. 'Hold on, Tom. Hold on,' she whispered, as they put him on a gurney and took him to the ambulance. She held his hand the whole way to the hospital, relinquishing him only when the doctors had to take him into surgery. 'I can't lose you now that I've found you.'

Maree spent the night in the hospital waiting room while Tom was in surgery. She was aware of Allegra and Carter taking turns to be with her, but her whole body vibrated with need to hear he was going to be all right. A doctor finally appeared in the doorway. 'The surgery went well.' The doctor smiled. 'He has months of recovery ahead of him, but there will be no lasting damage.'

Maree's legs gave out and Carter had to help her to a chair. Carter smooth-talked the doctor and Maree spent the night in Tom's hospital room, watching him as he slept. She'd been so close to losing him, but the universe was giving them another chance. She was so thankful.

Epilogue

One year later

Tom sat in the back of the limousine, admiring the stunning brunette sitting next to him. 'Come here, Mrs. Calvert.' He leaned down and kissed her on the lips.

He kept his hands on her waist, the smooth satin of her dress reminding him of the smooth skin beneath the soft material, but he knew better than to lift his hands to her hair. It had taken her four hours to get ready, because he had managed to seduce her into his bed for three of them.

'Mrs. Reynard-Calvert,' Maree corrected as she pushed him away and straightened her dress.

He lifted her hand to his lips and gently kissed it. He couldn't believe that it was a year ago he'd been shot.

He remembered waking up in hospital. He'd forced his eyes open. The beeping of machines had filled his ears. He'd felt someone touching his hand and looked down. A figure swam into focus. A woman was lying on a cot beside him, her hand holding his. He'd recognized the brown silky hair. 'Maree.'

She'd stirred and sat up, looking at him with tired eyes. 'Tom, you came back to me.'

'I told you I always would.'

'I thought I'd lost you.' She leaned across and gently hugged him, her tears falling on his neck.

'I'm here and I'm always going to stay by your side,' he'd said.

Maree cupped his cheek. 'Good.' She'd smiled, her brown eyes glowing with happiness.

Diane was supposed to go to trial, but was found mentally incompetent and placed in a psychiatric institution. Diane's ex-husband was a lawyer and had hired her the best counsel possible. To Tom's relief they had managed to win the motion to suppress the identity of the celebrity involved in the stalking scandal. While there had been rumors, of course, that Tom was the celebrity, nothing was proven. Carter had managed to sell the burglary gone wrong angle.

This had given Tom a much-needed reprieve to win Maree. Three months after the shooting he was released from hospital. His first night out he'd asked Maree out on a date. Even though she'd been quite happy to skip over the courtship rituals, he'd wanted to do everything right and woo her the old fashioned way and put to rest any doubts she had about their future together. For their first date he took her to Becossa, the restaurant he'd taken her to as Beau. He told her all the things he'd wanted to tell her then, but couldn't while he was in character.

Six months later, production on *Ten Steps to the Moon* commenced and they finally got to work together; more importantly Maree got her dream job. After the wrap party he'd arranged for a surprise weekend getaway at Carter's cabin where he recreated their first romantic night together. That was the night he proposed and she said yes. Their wedding was a private affair. Maree had been undecided about having her father and his family there, but Tom had convinced her to send them an invite. He'd made sure to have a strong chat to his future father-in-law about expectations of privacy, and there had been no surprise leaks to the media.

'We're nearly there.' Maree looked out the window.

Tom heard the roar of the crowd as they approached the Royale Theatre where the movie premiere was to be held. He knew the paparazzi could see through the tinted windows by using the flash of their cameras, so he didn't kiss her again. While there had been an announcement via the entertainment outlets about their wedding, this was their first public outing as newlyweds. He knew Maree's reluctance to be in the public eye and had tried to dissuade her from attending the premiere, but she wouldn't listen.

'This movie brought us together and I'm going to be there with you to witness your triumph,' she'd said, her hand over his scar. He called it her nervous tic. It was like she needed to touch the place where the bullet tore through him in order to remind herself that he was still breathing and wouldn't be stopping any time soon.

The car pulled up. 'This is it,' he said, his nerves taking over.

He had dreamed about this day for so long, but now that it was here he wanted to tell the driver to keep driving and take his beautiful bride home. Once they set foot onto the red carpet as a couple, things would never be the same.

'Are you ready for this?' he asked.

She gently kissed him on the lips, unheeding of the camera flashes lighting up the car and capturing their private kiss. 'I can't wait to stand beside my talented husband.'

He leaned his head forward and touched their foreheads together. Taking a deep breath he opened the car door and the roar of the crowd surrounded him. This was what he'd been waiting for all his life—the moment when he was transformed from a soap star slash model into a serious actor, yet now that it was here, all he cared about was the woman whose hand he was holding.

He looked down at her, concerned about how she was coping with the limelight, but Maree stepped out without hesitation, smiling as she held onto his arm. He could see that she was aware of the flashing cameras, but she didn't care. She turned toward the journalists and stood by his side, posing effortlessly. He curved his arm around her waist, his hand splayed over her still flat stomach.

After the photographers finished, they walked down the red carpet. Carter broke through the crowd and approached them. 'You look gorgeous, Maree.' He leaned forward and air kissed her cheek, knowing not to ruin the carefully applied makeup.

'Where's Allegra?' Maree asked.

Tom had arranged for Carter to be Allegra's escort.

'She's making the acquaintance of the latest Calvin Klein model.'

'I'll go find her.' Maree gave Tom's arm a squeeze and entered the theatre.

Carter stood by Tom's side and pointed up at the marquee above them where Tom's name was lit up in lights. 'Take it all in, my friend.'

The marketing plan to keep the lead actor's identity a secret had been instrumental in ensuring that *Heroes of Tennessee* was the talked about movie of the season. Tom's name had only been leaked when the trailer hit the movie screens and the word-of-mouth buzz had crescendoed into a roar.

'You mark my words, there will be an Oscar nomination out of this.' Carter slapped his back.

Tom nodded. He believed Carter, the movie was that good. It was a Ken Grey production and like all the others before it, this movie too would enter the Hollywood Hall of Fame.

His life was everything he had dreamed about a year ago when he had devised his so-called brilliant plan to live Beau's life and take on the role of his lifetime. He couldn't have known then that the only role that would matter to him was that of husband and father. While acting was his career and passion, Maree and their soon-to-be-born baby were his life.

About Author

 Mae Archer knew she wanted to be a writer since she was a child. She loved listening to her grandmother's war stories about English maidens falling in love with handsome Yankees while England burnt under the Luftwaffe's blitz.

When she discovered romance novels as a teenager she soon realised that her dream job was to be a romance writer. After many career twists and turns she's making her dreams come true.

Mae's real life is like one of her grandmother's stories. She met a foreigner who travelled through Australia and it was love at first sight. She married him six months after they met and every day since has been an adventure. She lives in Australia with her husband and daughter.

Mae has been an avid reader of romance novels since she was a teenager and her own novels combine some of her favourite romance tropes including time travel, second chances and star-crossed lovers.

Mae Archer is the pen name for author Amra Pajalic. Amra writes young adult contemporary fiction under her own name and dark fiction as A.P. Pajalic.

SIGN UP FOR AMRA'S AUTHOR NEWSLETTER

For news, giveaways, bonus material, and sneak peeks, please sign up to her newsletter below.

www.amrapajalic.com

CONNECT WITH AMRA

goodreads.com/author/show/3310015.Amra_Pajalic

facebook.com/AmraPajalicAuthor/

instagram.com/amrapajalicauthor/

https://twitter.com/AmraPajalic

bookbub.com/authors/amra-pajalic

tiktok.com/@amrapajalic

youtube.com/c/AmraPajalicAuthor

CONNECT WITH MAE

www.maearcherromance.com

https://twitter.com/MaeArcher12

goodreads.com/mae_archer

facebook.com/MaeArcherRomance

PLEASE LEAVE A REVIEW

If you enjoyed this book and would like to show Amra your support, please consider leaving a star rating and/or review on the website you purchased the book from.

Dreams of Destiny

Dreams of Destiny series are suspense novels featuring lovers who are each searching for a dream, when love finds them at the most inconvenient time. They feature secret identities, hidden agendas and thwarted ambition.

You've already met Tom and Maree in the first book of the series. Book 2 features Maree's best friend, Allegra, and book 3 is about Gerald 'Mack' Mackevoy as we discover what he's doing impersonating a homeless person.

Hollywood Dreams

She's fallen for his greatest role. But can she fall for him?

Vintage Dreams

She had to nearly die before she could live again. Can she build a new life on the embers of her old one?

Vengeful Dreams

She's dreamt of vengeance since she was a young girl. Can she find redemption in love?

Vintage Dreams

She had to nearly die before she could live again. Can she build a new life on the embers of her old one?

After being diagnosed with breast cancer Allegra Kenton finds new direction using her passion for vintage items by renovating a dilapidated mansion she inherited into a dance studio. When she meets Emmett Dennison and begins falling in love it seems that her new life is on track, until a mistake from her past puts everything in jeopardy. Can she hold onto her dreams and Emmett?

Emmett Dennison had a plan: the right type of fiancé, the right time to get married, the right career rung, but his plan took a detour when he became a guardian to his autistic brother and his fiancé broke off their engagement. Now his life is all about the day to day, until he meets Allegra. She inspires him to dream again, but his fiancé's betrayal makes it hard for him to trust. Will Allegra make him believe in happy endings?

Return to Me

A fatal accident. A parallel world. Second chances don't come often.

Death has never been far from Lana. In a previous life, her husband Frank died from a heart condition at thirty. In this new world where she's known as Alannah Walker, it's Tristan by her side as husband, and he had a heart operation as a child. But that's where the similarities end between them.

Born Frank Walters, Tristan hides his past under a new name. His relationship with his wife, Alannah, fraught with anger. Alannah has seemed like a different person since the car accident, and lessons of the past have taught him not to trust too easily.

Will Tristan and Lana learn enough from past mistakes to give them a second chance at love?

Be transported to another world on a breathtaking ride into the unknown, where two lovers will come to find the true meaning of forever. *Return to Me* is a heart wrenching tale of love, loss, and rediscovery that will draw you in from the very first page

Buy *Return to Me* now and lose yourself in a world where second chances make anything possible.

Also By

Romance as Mae Archer

Return to Me

Hollywood Dreams

Memoir

Things Nobody Knows But Me

Growing up Muslim in Australia

Young Adult

The Cuckoo's Song

Sabiha's Dilemma

Alma's Loyalty

The Climb

Dark Fiction/Horror as A.P. Pajalic

Woman on the Edge